VULCAN'S KITTENS

BOOK 1 OF CHILDREN OF MYTH

CEDAR SANDERSON

For my eldest daughter, who asked for this book.

SUMMER VACATION

*L*innea looked out the tiny window of the tiny plane and marveled at the mountains below it. They had flown out of the Boise airport just a half hour before, but already she could see few signs of civilization below them. Her trip had started out that morning, in the Seattle Airport. She leaned her head against the cool window glass and re-lived the earlier scene with her mother.

"Mom, I'll be fine. I want you to do this." She'd insisted.

Her mother had hugged her, and Linnaea had leaned into her comfortable bulk, smelling the scent of lilacs and roses her mother always wore. Theta Vulkane was a renowned photographer, and traveled the world taking pictures of volcanoes and forest fires. But for the last two years she had stayed home with her only daughter. When this assignment had come in Linnaea could see how much her mother wanted to go.

"Dad and I, we had a lot of fun when you were gone. He always wanted you to go. Just because he's not here..." Linnaea tried to keep her lip from wobbling. She took a deep breath and went on. "I'm sure Grampa Heff can keep me out of trouble."

"Oh, I know he can. He always kept me from getting into too much. He's just,

well, since your grandmother left, he is sad and a bit cranky."

"Mom, it's not like I don't have your phone number. And a new phone - thank you so much!"

Reminded of that in the present, Linn sat up and pulled it out of her jacket pocket. Her mom had always resisted her getting a phone - no amount of teasing and begging had moved her for the last two years, since she had gone into sixth grade and most of her friends had gotten one. But in the whirlwind of packing and preparation her mother had bought her the latest smart phone and loaded it with games and ebooks. Linn suspected the gift was partly to atone for the abandonment.

She didn't care though. It was cool. She texted her mother now, making sure she didn't use text speak. Mom would explode if she did, so she wrote, "Almost there. Flying over Nez Perce Mountains."

She played a game, and then, bored, switched to her ebooks. Her mom had loaded the Diaries of Lewis and Clark onto it, no doubt hoping that she would get interested in the history of the area her grandfather lived in. Linn decided she would read that later and opened the latest fantasy novel instead. It was really cool, about how the gods of myth and folklore were living among humans and hiding their abilities. She read happily until they were on final approach to the Pierce Airport.

Grampa Heff was waiting for her in the little terminal, which was barely the two rooms needed for TSA regulations. He was leaning on his cane, she noticed. She ran to him and hugged him fiercely, which made him snort and lean into her. He smelled of smoke and apple tobacco, which made her sneeze.

He grinned at her when she finally let go. "Ready for a summer with an old coot?"

"Yep. I'm planning to be bored and whiny already. "

"Oh, I remember your mother at this age. Whew. Her moods could change on a dime."

Linn grimaced. She did that too. Frustrating. She'd talked to Mom about it, and although she understood that partly it was her body and hormones and all that, it was still annoying to start crying for no reason at all. Or yelling at her mother.

"I'll try to be good, Grampa."

Despite the cane, her grandfather was as strong as the steel that was his trade. He pitched her bags into the back of the truck and climbed into the cab beside her.

"Want to tool around town before we head up to the farm. Need to pick up some groceries. I also remember how much your mom ate at your age."

Linn sighed. Her mom wouldn't let her diet, either. Women in her family were supposed to be all 'generous curves' according to her, and no, Linn wasn't fat at all. No matter what her friends said. She had a pretty good idea of what her grandfather would say if she asked for diet food. She helped shop at the grocery store, a very small place, nothing like the massive city supermarkets she was used to. Her grandfather bought a lot of stuff in bulk.

"We'll have a garden for veggies," he explained. "And I have a freezer full of meat, so this is mostly staples for the next month. Your Mom said you like to cook and bake?"

"We aren't coming back to town for a month?"

"Well, maybe. I don't come to town much."

Linn blinked up at him, speechless for a moment. Yes, Pierce was a one-horse town, but the idea of not going anywhere for a month had surprised her. Where she lived in Seattle she could walk to the library, or to meet her friends.

"OK." She finally said, realizing there wasn't much to do in Pierce anyway. No wonder her mom had bought the phone for her. And no point in arguing with Grandpa Heff. His stubbornness was legendary.

The ride up to his farm was quiet. Linn spent most of it looking out the window admiring the scenery as they climbed up into the mountains. At one point her grandfather pulled over onto the side of the road and she got out and stared in awe at the perfect meadow of wildflowers in front of her. Her grandfather cleared his throat. "The blue ones are Camas. Kinda gets you, don't it?"

"Wow, Grampa, it's so beautiful."

The field reached out endlessly, it seemed. The flowers were as blue as the sky above them, and for a moment she felt like she was floating between sky and sky. The scattered reds and yellows among the river of blue were like rays of sunlight coming through cracks. The scent of the flowers filled her up and she closed her eyes, savoring the warmth on her face. She looked back, realizing that she'd walked a little way out into the field. Her grandfather just leaned against the truck, his arms crossed and a small smile on his face.

Linn took a couple of pictures and climbed back in the truck. "Thanks, Grampa."

"Thank you, young lady. Helps me see it fresh again through your eyes." Without taking his eyes off the road, he reached over and ruffled her hair.

When they pulled into the farmyard the chickens scattered from the truck and then gathered again as soon as the engine was off. Linn hopped out and reached in for her bags, but her grandfather waved her off.

"Got a surprise for you in the barn. See if you can find it."

Linn started for his small barn. Grampa didn't keep any large livestock, so the barn was just big enough for a couple goats and their hay. As she got to the sliding doors, she saw the cat sitting on the stump beside them. Sitting upright, tail curled around her toes, she was a very elegant tawny cat.

"Hello, pretty lady." Linn held out her hand to be sniffed. The cat surveyed her for a moment, and then leaped off the stump to wait at the doors. Linn was surprised at the size of her, fully as tall as her knee. The softly weaving tail, tip hooked like a shepherd's crook at the moment, reached up to her waist. Linn slid the door open and the cat walked into the dimness of the barn. Linn could smell the sweet hay in the loft. The cat turned back and said firmly "Mew."

Linn chuckled. "I am coming, Cat."

The cat ascended to the loft in two swift bounds, one to the top of the stall door and the other to the floor of the loft, easily ten feet above them. Linn was impressed, but stopped to rub the noses of Grandpa's two Alpine does as they stood in the stall. Then the cat miaowed again, and Linn obediently climbed the ladder to the loft. The cat sat on a bale of hay looking down into a little cavity surrounded by four bales on the floor. Linn looked into it.

"Kittens! Oh, how precious!"

She knelt on the floor and reached over the bale toward them, then hesitated. "May I?" she asked the mother cat. This was a very dignified beast, and very different from the house cats Linn knew at home. The cat curled her paws under her chest and began to purr, eyes half lidded. Linn took this to mean yes, and stroked the top of the nearest kitten's head.

"You are so soft." She murmured, not wanting to disturb the sleepy kittens. There were four of them. One black, one calico, and two silvery gray with black spots. They bobbed blind little heads at her and opened little pink mouths in soundless mews, but Linn could see they would be even bigger than their mother, as they were already the size of her two fists put together, and they couldn't be more than two weeks old.

Linn stroked each of the kittens for a few minutes, marveling at the soft fur and cute round tummies. She stopped when their mother flowed into the nest and wrapped herself around them. The kittens immediately nosed into her teats. Even blind they knew exactly where to go. Linn sighed. This was a very nice surprise.

"Linn? Dinnertime." Her grandfather sounded like he was calling from the porch.

"Coming, Grampa." She called back, no longer worried about waking the kittens.

She climbed down the ladder and washed up at the pump between the house and the smithy. Her grandfather had designed the pump and basin to overflow into a koi pond, and she trailed her fingers in it to feel the eager mouths nibble at her.

Dinner was a venison stew and rustic bread. Her grandfather was a good cook. She sighed a little, looking down at her half empty bowl. Her father had been a good cook, too.

After dinner her grandfather pointed to the loft. "Up you go! These old knees can't do the ladder, but you'll be sleeping up there this summer, unless you decide to sleep in the barn."

"Could I?" Linn asked, picturing the kittens.

"Not tonight, but yes. Now bed. "

Linn fell asleep quickly, worn out with her long day of traveling. In the middle of the night, she woke up with the familiar feeling of a crampy stomach. Her period had started. Yuck. She rolled over to get out of bed and then realized that there was someone in the cabin talking to Grampa Heff.

"You do realize you cannot stay out of this forever." A heavy male voice, dripping with anger and a strange accent.

"We choose to treat Hephaestus as a refuge." A sibilant and melodious female voice. Linn thought she had a speech impediment.

Linn crawled out of bed, her belly cramps forgotten and slid to the edge of the loft where she could see into the sitting area below. Four figures stood down there in the dimly lit room. The two closest to the door were very big. If they walked under the loft they would have to duck. The one on the couch appeared to be huddled under Grampa's afghan. Grampa Heff himself was straddling a kitchen chair he had turned backwards and was leaning his crossed arms on the back of it.

"Vulcan - ah, Haephestus, as you prefer. You choose to live unnaturally. We would rather not force you to return with us."

"I chose to make myself happy, not your lot. And do you recall what happened last time I was forced?"

Linn could see a grimace pass over the man's face. In the firelight his skin was unusually red, as was his hair. She wondered why Grampa hadn't lit a lamp.

"I cannot and will not leave here." The woman on the couch declared, sitting up suddenly. Linn startled as she realized that the woman was a cat... This was her grandfather's barn cat, talking and sitting on the couch.

The big man stepped toward her, casting his face into shadow. Linn could still hear the sneer in his voice. "Bastet's Daughter, you are the least of our concerns. Vulcan may take on strays and broken... beings, but we do not."

"I would not go with you, even without my obligations here." Grampa interjected.

"Oh, the child." The man's dismissive tone made Linn's blood boil.

"Not just a child. Blood of my blood."

"Which I'm sure she knows nothing about. To her, you are just a broken-down old smith."

"Her mother has told her what we are, I am certain."

"She could not even see me if she were able to wake from the spell I cast over her."

Linn blinked in surprise. Not only was she wide awake, riveted to the conversation below, but she could see the red man, the cat woman, and the bulk of something else (she was no longer sure it was a man) near the door in the shadows. And as for 'what she was'... she was a human being. Wasn't she? Linn remembered her mother once telling her that not all myths and fairy tales were made up. Many of the old tales had a grain of truth in them.

"There are very powerful things in this world of ours, things that most people cannot see or accept if they do see them." Theta's voice had gone dreamy, and Linn saw that her eyes were focused somewhere far away. "My family is a powerful one, and you have a little of that power, my sweet. If you see strange things, or feel like you did something you cannot explain, then I will tell you more."

Linn dragged her attention back to the scene below. Her mother wasn't there to explain, but she knew who she was going to talk to as soon as their visitors left.

"I think the child will surprise you, Mars." Grampa Heff's voice was mild. Linn suddenly caught the connection of names. Mars and Vulcan were gods. Bastet was the cat god of Egypt. Who were these people? Who was her grandfather? Linn felt dizzy even lying flat on the floor.

"In any case," Her grandfather stood up and Linn could see the fire shimmering through his halo of white hair. She suddenly wondered what color it had been when he was young. "You will leave now. I have no intention of abandoning my work."

"You will come to Olympus."

"You can't make me."

"Oh, I have ways..." Mars backed out of the door. His unseen bodyguard had already gone out.

Grampa Heff sighed and ran his hands through his hair, making it stand even more on end. He looked up toward Linn. "Come on down, child."

Lid slid down the ladder. "How did you know?"

He chuckled and hugged her. "I could hear you breathing, little one. How much did you hear?"

Linn realized he was asking her how much she had really understood. "Not much... why did he call you Vulcan? Where did he want you to go? Was he really red?"

Her grandfather laughed. "Vulcan is one of my names, the gods are meeting to arrange the fate of the world and he is indeed, red."

"The fate of the world? Gods? What?" Her dizzy feeling came back.

"Sit, child." Bastet's Daughter, forgotten behind her, reached out a soft and very large paw to pull her down onto the couch. Linn sank down next to the warm bulk of the cat, who was now closer to tiger-sized.

"You grew." Linn muttered.

The cat laughed.

Grampa Heff smiled. "I think we need to explain, but first, hot cocoa."

"He wanted you to come with him and leave me here?"

"The gods care naught for mortals." The cat yawned, showing her pink tongue and very long fangs. "I am only a goddess, so I do care." She licked Linn's cheek. "Kittens and children are to be cherished."

"A goddess?" Linn felt like some of her skin was missing. That was a very rough tongue.

"I am daughter of Bastet, sometimes known as Bast, I am known as Hathor and Sekhmet. I have the power to walk among mortals seeming as a mere housecat. I am also a god."

"God is a misnomer, Sekhmet." Grampa Heff corrected.

"True, but it amuses me." Her chuckle morphed into a purr that shook Linn.

"Here you are," he handed Linn a steaming mug of cocoa with marshmallows bobbing in it. She sipped gratefully at the rich, sweet liquid. "Mortals call us gods, but the truth is, we are simply immortal beings that can learn and last long enough to seem like magic to those who have not the gift of long life."

"But you can do magic. Mars said he had cast a spell."

"Well..." he hesitated. "It isn't precisely magic."

The cat snorted. "Close enough to pass for it."

He sighed. "True. So, yes, I can do magic. As you can at least a little."

"Me?" Linn squeaked.

"You were awake, watching, and listening. So yes, you can see much more than a mere mortal could."

"But I must be about... a quarter, um, whatever you are?"

He shook his head. "Your mother is fully immortal. Your grandmother is immortal, and a child of two immortals is one. You are half mortal."

Linn blinked. "Why did.... Mars come to summon you?"

"The immortals are growing afraid of the mortals. They believe that unless technology is stopped, the mortals will achieve what they have already - power."

"I don't think they can stop technology."

"They can." He said grimly, getting that faraway look on his face that her mother sometimes wore. "They have done it before. Humanity would have come much further if it were not for the Great Falls of civilization."

"Oh."

He rubbed his face and sighed. "I was looking forward to a quiet summer vacation with you."

"And I to raising my kittens in peace." Sekhmet muttered.

Linn looked back and forth between the two of them. "Can you... stop them?"

Heff shrugged. "There are more than the two of us that care about mortals. We can stop them if we can persuade all to work together, but I am afraid it will be messy."

He looked at the Cat, who was curled mostly around Linn. Linn's eyes were drooping in spite of herself as the warm, softly furred creature purred to her.

"Sekhmet, can I ask you to go and speak to those who have assumed beast form?"

"My kittens?" She reminded him gently.

"Well, I think we can supply a babysitter." He looked at the child, half asleep already.

"True." the amusement was back in her voice. Linn thought drowsily that the cat must have a great sense of humor, she always seemed to be laughing, or about to chuckle. They may have talked more, but Linn didn't hear it, being fast asleep.

2

KITTEN DUTY

*L*inn woke up in the morning to her grandfather shaking her shoulder. "Get up, girl, you have kittens to feed."

"Whah?" She sat up and rubbed her eyes. She was on the couch, covered in the afghan. Sekhmet was nowhere to be seen. For a fleeting second, she wondered if she had dreamed it all.

"Kittens need feeding. Sekhmet left last night, she filled their tummies before she went, but now it's up to you."

"Oh!" Linn sat straight up. "How do I do that?"

"Bottle of warm goat milk." He pointed at a milk crate by the door. "Tonight, you get to fill them, but you had a long night last night."

"Thank you, Grampa." She scrambled out of the tangle of afghan and headed for the loft and day clothes.

"Thermos is for you. Hurry now - they are crying."

Linn could hear them when she got into the barn. Little sonic shrieks, so high she almost couldn't make them out. Getting the milk crate up the ladder was difficult, and when she got her head above the floor, she could see that all four kittens were trying to climb out of their hay bale corral. She scrambled up and patted heads. The black one sucked on her finger while she fumbled for a bottle with the other hand.

"How am I supposed to feed all of you at once?" She muttered.

She compromised by taking them out one at a time and holding them in her lap to feed. They were bigger than she remembered, even from last night, and she thought their mother must have been keeping her from seeing the reality when she first met them. Two of them - the black one and the calico - had their eyes open just a little. Full tummies meant nap time, and she cuddled the spotted one that had been last fed while the other slept in a boneless heap in their corral.

Her grandfather came in and looked up at her. "How goes it?"

"They are full. Two have their eyes open. Do they have names?"

He shrugged. "You can call them whatever you want, cats usually have several names. Their mother won't mind."

"When will she be back?"

"I don't know."

"Is she in any danger?"

He sighed. "Come on down, I'm getting a crick in my neck."

"Grampa, last night, Mars called you Hephaestus and Vulcan. And Sekhmet is an Egyptian goddess."

He tousled her hair. "Right. I have many names. As do most immortals. We live long enough with mortals, and they start to call us gods. Then, each different culture, like the Greeks and Romans, has different names for us."

"So, all the gods of myth were really immortals? And why don't people now still worship you?"

"Well, they don't worship me because I don't want them to. Never really did. Other immortals... well. A few centuries back there was a war. Spilled over down to the mortals, sadly, but the long-term effect was they stopped worshipping us. Started to look beyond us to realize that the Universe is a helluva lot bigger than these petty gods they had set up, and there had to be more. There are still isolated cultures that believe, and corrupt immortals that encourage that, but the civilized world has moved on."

Linn thought this might be the most she'd ever heard her grandfather talk.

"You were part of that, weren't you."

He looked down at her. He wasn't all that much taller than she was, any more, and his craggy, bearded face hid the lopsidedness that was his downfall from Olympus in the first place.

"Maybe." was all he said.

"I love you, Gramps." Linn hugged him. "So, what do we do now?"

"Lunch."

Linn sensed she wasn't going to get more out of him right then.

They ate in silence, and then he sent her back out to the kittens, with an armful of bedding. She was going to sleep in the loft with them that night. Linn amused herself with trying out names for them.

"Athena?" she picked up the calico and inspected the little blunt faced kitten. The tiny ears were more rounded than a regular kitten's would be.

Her grandfather's voice came up from below where he was milking the goats. "She wouldn't be pleased to have a kitten named for her."

"Grampa, why are their ears round?"

"Their father is a Mayan god. The Jaguar God of Terrestrial Fire."

"I prefer to be called Steve." Another voice entered into their conversation. His voice was slightly accented. Linn looked down from the loft at a slender black-haired man. He looked up at her and smiled. "Ah, the child who watches my kittens. Buenos Dias, Senorita."

"You aren't a cat." Linn blurted. Then she blushed, she could feel the heat of it from her chest to her ears. "I'm sorry."

"No, child, you are correct. I do not wear my beast image in public. It helps in this oh-so modern world."

"Steve, what brings you here?"

"Well, Heff, I hear there's going to be trouble."

Her grandfather snorted. "And when there's trouble, there you are."

Steve shrugged. "Perhaps. I wanted your thoughts on this. Sekhmet did not have time to chat."

Heff sighed. "Let me finish with the milking. Your kits will be cranky if they aren't fed."

"Of course." He looked back up at Linn. "May I come up, O guardian?"

Linn giggled. The very dignified man swarmed up the ladder effortlessly. He stood at the top and bowed elegantly to her.

"I wanted to thank you for keeping them safe." He told her gravely. She had never met anyone as mercurial as him, grave one moment and laughing the next.

"I like kittens, and they are so sweet."

He sat on a bale and tickled the black kitten's chin. "He looks just like me."

"What is his name?"

"Oh, I don't know. I haven't seen them before this."

Linn gaped at him. He laughed. "I am a cat, *chica*."

"As for names..." he bent over the awakened kittens. All their eyes were open now, but they didn't track very well. "How about Blackie, Spot, Patches and Spot?"

Linn laughed. "No! They deserve better than that."

"Well, then, I shall leave it in your capable hands, young lady."

"Right now, she needs to come down and fill up bottles." Heff's voice rose from below them.

"Coming Grampa." She called back.

Linn climbed down the ladder and took the milk pail from him. Steve followed her down and went with her grandfather into the house. Linn filled kitten bottles and raised them in the pulley basket her grandfather had rigged that afternoon. Much better than trying to climb up the ladder with them.

The hay loft was quiet as she fed the kittens, with only the faint squeaks of the siblings that weren't being fed audible. Linn decided that the black kitten was the boldest. Certainly, the greediest, she thought as she pulled the bottle away from him. She took the smallest, spotted one out of their enclosure to feed as Blackie showed signs of pushing him away from the bottle and taking it for himself.

"Enough, piggie boy." She scolded him. He flipped onto his back and waved his front paws at her. Linn rubbed his full tummy.

"I need to learn more about your parents before I give you names. I wonder if Grampa has some books about the mythology of Egypt and Mexico." She sighed. Having no internet slowed research down a lot.

Spots was asleep in her lap, and purring loudly enough to vibrate her to her bones. Linn leaned against the hay bales. It was warm and smelled good up here. The hay was a little scratchy in places, but she was sleepy enough to ignore that and relax fully. She closed her eyes and drifted into the warmth.

3

SOMETIMES KNOWN AS VULCAN

*H*ephaestus, sometimes known as Vulcan, and more recently as Heff Vulkane, stood looking at his house and barn from the dark edge of the woods. He was walking the perimeter, renewing the wards that would warn him of intruders to his little domain. He'd known Mars was coming, but had wanted to hear out the angry god's spiel. Heff sighed. With the girl and kittens to protect, his hands were tied. Traveling would be difficult at best for a while.

He had, perhaps, waited too long already. In the two weeks since Sekhmet had gone, the kittens had grown and developed amazingly. But the news that was filtering back to him led him to believe that the gods were moving fast, this time. The last time they had been slow, too complicated.

"No plan survives contact with the enemy." He muttered to himself.

The warm light spilling from the open barn door reminded him that Linn hadn't had dinner. He made his way back to the barn, walking in shadows until he reached the cleared field of fire around the buildings, and then he walked cautiously, aware of his exposure. They might not come for him. But they probably would. He was too well known as the outsider, the immortal who loved humans.

He climbed the ladder to the hayloft and stood with a smile on his face looking down at the little heap of kittens and girl, fast asleep. The kittens had climbed out of their nest and were lying near or on Linn. She had a half-smile on her face. Heff thought she looked a lot like her grandmother at the moment. He tucked a strand of silky black hair behind her ear and out of her face.

He missed his wife, but it had been complicated. Right at this moment he couldn't remember what it was that complicated things, and he wished she were here to help him understand what was happening, and how to protect the children.

Her blanket was gripped in one hand, and he remembered the little stuffed cat she had carried about for years, until it was rags and a memory. He wondered where it had been stored. Theta would have saved it, he was certain. His daughter's wandering feet kept her from collecting many possessions, but she loved this little girl to her bones. When Mark had died, it had almost killed her. The only thing that had saved her from the lonely fate of so many immortals had been the little girl who was part of both of them.

He left the barn and sat on the bench in the shadows, pulling out his pipe and lighting it slowly, thinking.

Night was falling quickly, and the temperature was dropping in the clear air of the mountains. Even in the summer it got cold at night. He didn't mind. After the heat of the forge it was refreshing, and he didn't feel the cold. He'd always loved the mountains, where the extremes of nature fought with humans struggling for existence on their slopes. It was in his early years that they had won his admiration with their sheer persistence. In time, that had come to an abiding desire to protect all humans, struggling uphill against the gods.

The children of the gods were particularly precious. He had several right here in his barn. That thought made him chuckle in a cloud of exhaled pipe smoke. The snobs on Olympus would have a fit if they knew. They considered themselves royalty.

Heff heaved a huge sigh. Those sleepy children wouldn't be alone for too long while he went to rally the mortal lovers to his side, to fight again for the right of humanity to grow unchecked. He wasn't going to allow a second Dark Age to fall like this night had fallen on his mountain.

"I need a babysitter for them." He mused finally. The problem was, who could he trust to keep an eye on them for a few days while he ran errands?

4

DANGER CLOSE

*L*inn yawned hugely and shifted a kitten off her chest, where his weight was making it hard to breathe. Although their guise of house cat size was good, they weighed more than you would expect. No way to hide mass, she thought sleepily. The kitten stretched out and put his paw gently on her nose, then relaxed back into sleep.

She could hear Grampa below, milking the goats. She needed to learn to do that, she remembered. Extricating herself from the kittens, she climbed down the ladder. He looked at her, then nodded for her to come sit down on the stool as he stood, milk pail in his hands.

"Don't leave this near their feet." He cautioned as she was seated, handing it back to her. "They'll kick it over and you'll lose your hard work, and the kitten's breakfast."

She nodded and put it carefully back under the doe's teats. The goat ignored her, munching on the grain in front of her, weight shifted to her far side and standing perfectly still.

Heff grunted. "Silly here is a good girl. She's patient, so it will be easy to learn on her. Put your hand around her teat, like that..." he showed her how to wrap her hand around it, thumb at the top. "Squeeze from the top down. Lock the milk in with your thumb and forefinger, otherwise the milk will just go back into the udder. Don't worry about hurting her, girl, her kids wouldn't - and they have teeth before long, too."

Linn squeezed down, finger by finger as he'd taught her, and was rewarded by a thin stream of milk... right onto her pants leg. Heff laughed. "Aim for the bucket, girl."

She did and heard the tinny splash of the milk hitting the pail. "All right, now try both hands." She had a little trouble with the rhythm of two hands at once, until he explained that one hand at a time, one after the other was the usual way.

"Don't try to use both hands at once."

Linn leaned her cheek against the goat's warm belly, hearing the rumen grumble inside it, and concentrated on milking the patient doe. Her hands started to cramp.

"Ouch." She rubbed her palm.

"Enough for your first lesson. Go on now." Heff's voice was amused from where he was leaning on the gate.

Linn remembered to hand him the bucket and got up. He sat in her place and said, "Here, this is how to strip her out and make sure she's done. You need to make sure you do this, or she could get an infection."

He milked Silly for a minute, his quick rhythm a counterpoint to Linn's hesitant streams. The he showed her the flaccid teat.

"Nearly there. Bump your hand up into the udder..." he did this as he spoke. "Like her kid would do, asking for another sip. She'll let down the last of it."

He stripped out the last milk and stood, handing the pail to Linn. "Get this in the house while I milk Sally. This pail's ours. Put it in the icebox in the jars. Make sure you run it through the filter. "

She nodded and headed to the house. The milk was a prime environment for bacteria to grow in, so it had to be chilled as quickly as possible. Otherwise, it would smell and taste funny. As it was, she always had to get used to the rich thickness of it compared to the 2% milk her mom bought for her at home.

She rinsed the pail and left it in the sink. Her Grampa would sterilize it with the rest of the equipment when he was finished. When she got back out to the barn, Heff was up in the loft. He looked down at her.

"Stay put a minute. I'm going to try and get them corralled up here better..." he grunted and she saw that he was unrolling chicken wire across the opening in the loft. "Send up that staple gun, won't you?"

She put it in the basket and pulled it up to him. He took it out of the basket and pointed to the milking stand. "Get those bottles filled while I do this."

She went obediently to the milk and could hear the tack of the staples above her while she readied four bottles and twisted on the rubber nipples. The wire would keep the kittens from falling out of the loft, she guessed. She wondered why he wanted to keep them in the barn. She'd like to take them in the house.

Up in the hayloft, Hephaestus was wondering when she would ask him that. His reason, of course, would be difficult to explain to her. He knew she'd understand it a little, but the millennia-old vows still held, and it was as good for him to adhere to them as it was for the enemy... he frowned to himself. When had he started to think of them as the enemy? Must have been about 1893... when the information age had begun to accelerate into a threat to the old, established ways. When they had started not caring about mortals. Well, that had been going on for millennia, anyway.

He wrapped the ends of the wire back into itself at the gap for the ladder so neither girl nor kittens would be scratched. He would build a little gate separately and then hang it here in the opening. This wouldn't keep the kittens long, he knew, but long enough. Things were coming to a crisis point, but he hoped to be able to get the young ones to a safe place, at least. When the kittens could travel, which they couldn't, yet.

He looked down at the floor of the barn, where Linn was filling the last bottle. She was trying hard to do this right. He appreciated her care for the kittens. He also wished she were a little better prepared for what was coming. She hadn't yet manifested any talents that indicated if she had inherited his blood, but that didn't mean anything. Children of the gods were often late bloomers. He snorted. The early bloomers had historically met early demises, as well.

Heff climbed down the ladder easily. With Linn he need not pretend he felt aches and pains that a mortal of his apparent age would. And he had finally decided who to call on as babysitter. He needed to get out and do some campaigning, as much as he hated the idea, and he couldn't leave the children alone. Even if Linn would protest that designation. As she started up the ladder he reached out and touched her cheek.

Linn was startled when Grampa patted her cheek. It was unlike him to show affection. She looked at him and smiled. "I can take care of them."

"I know you can. I was just thinking how much like your grandmother you are."

"I miss her."

"I do too. Now get feeding while I make that gate."

Linn finished her ascent and laughed to find the kittens lined up waiting for her. "Silly little guys, you are always hungry!"

She started with Blackie and Patches, as usual, while the spot twins rolled around in the hay playing with one another, and one of her feet. Their claws were sharp, and she yelped when one of the kittens tried to climb up her back. She pulled the kitten off her back and looked at him sternly.

"Spot One, there will be consequences for not minding your manners!"

He blinked his big blue eyes at her and she kissed him on the nose, and then gave him his bottle. Blackie stretched out along her thigh and began to purr. His buzzing shook her whole body. She finished feeding the Spots and when they were asleep, slid Spot One off her lap onto Blackie, who opened one eye, licked his brother and went back to sleep. Spot Two was trying to wash herself, and Linn grabbed the damp cloth out of the basket and rubbed the kitten's face with it. Sekhmet usually did this for her kittens, baths and toilet. Linn was glad they were finally using the litter pan. She had been contemplating kitten diapers for a couple of days there; surely she could cut tail holes in regular ones.

Spot Two staggered over to her brothers and curled up with them. Linn rubbed Patches' belly and then scooted her closer to the kitten heap, too. Patches yawned, showing off her tiny, needle-sharp fangs.

Linn looked down to see where Heff was, but he was nowhere in sight. She looked at the sleepy kittens and decided they weren't going anywhere with their full round bellies. She climbed down the ladder and followed her nose into the house. Her grandfather was pulling a loaf of bread out of the oven.

"Stew's on." He pointed at the wood stove.

Linn grabbed a bowl and dished herself some. "It's good," she told him with her mouth full. She was starving. Heff grunted at her.

Linn ate silently for a few minutes, watching him roam around the house, picking things up and then putting them down again.

"Grampa, what's wrong?"

Heff sighed and walked over to the table. He tousled Linn's hair.

"I'm going to be leaving soon. I have to get out there and see what's going on. Meet some people. I've called in a babysitter for you."

Linn frowned. "I don't..."

He grandfather cut her off. "Yes, you do. There bad things happening."

"What is happening? I'm not a baby, Grampa, and I do need to know. I need to be ready."

Heff looked down at her for a long moment, one bushy eyebrow raised. She could see forever in his dark brown eyes. There was a flicker of something... He blinked, and was just her grandfather again. He sat down and looked at her.

"How much did you hear when Mars visited that night?"

"I heard that he wants you to join his side. He hates mortals, doesn't he?"

"He hates not being worshipped anymore. You've heard the term absolute power corrupts absolutely?"

"Yes."

"Well, that's what we immortals have. We cannot be killed."

"But even immortals could be killed. What happens if someone cuts off your head or burns you up?"

Heff laughed. "Book and TV vampires aren't immortal. They just live a really long time unless someone kills them. My people are truly immortal. And not human."

"Then what are you... um, and what about me?"

"I can't tell you. Can you trust me, princess?"

He hadn't called her that since she was small enough to sit in his lap, she wished she could do that now. Her head felt full. She nodded, after a

CEDAR SANDERSON

moment. She knew Grampa Heff would never hurt her, and if he said he couldn't tell her, he couldn't. She'd never known him to lie.

"All right then. You are half-blooded. You have a little of me, a little of your grandmother in you."

"Grandmother is an immortal?"

"Yes. She isn't with me because she feels responsible to her homeland, you know. Unlike me, she's put down roots and invested so much of herself there, she doesn't feel happy anywhere else."

"Can't you go there and be with her?"

Heff sighed and ran a hand through his hair. "I was trying to stay near you, but then..." He shrugged. "We'll see what happens."

"So who are the bad guys, Grampa? Why do the gods... the immortals, want to fight?"

"Some of us were happy to give up godhood. Some of us never wanted it in the first place. Also, the most powerful among us maintain a pure form, and look down on those who assume other guises."

"What?" Linn was confused.

"Beast shapes. When we were new to this plane, some of us were forced to abandon the preferred, human guise, and take on the shape of animals. I can't tell you why without explaining what we are. Just take it that the purists among us look down on beings like Sekhmet and Steve."

"That's not fair."

He shrugged. "I was raised by one. A water naiad. So to me, they're just folks and shouldn't be considered less than that."

"I should think not!" Linn was indignant at the idea of the big, gentle cat Sekhmet being considered unworthy.

"The other thing, my little girl, is that they consider humans... well, equivalent to pets. Or sometimes to pests. They feel threatened by the level of human knowledge right now. They have for about a century now, but they've been slow to see what I see."

"Which is?"

"That humanity may shortly have weapons that could kill even us."

"I thought you said..."

"Yes, I know, and it hasn't happened yet. But it's coming soon, and the balance of power will shift."

26

"Will that be a good thing?"

"I don't know, honey. I'd like to say yes."

"But you're worried."

"Yep, I am. They are going to be interesting times, and past experience..." His eyes shifted and she knew he was remembering, and she shivered a little at the knowledge that he'd been there through terrible times. "Well, a lot of people may die. Life won't be easy, like it is now."

"What can we do?"

Heff smiled at his pugnacious little granddaughter. Of all the children he'd helped raise over the millennia, she was his favorite. He'd long given over mourning the mayfly intensity of life and death among humans, and settled into enjoying the glorious beauty of their existence. This one delighted him.

"You do nothing but watch over the kittens. I have to go, but you aren't ready to join the fight, yet."

Linn thrust out her lower lip. "I can help somehow."

"You are. Keeping the children safe means we continue. Losing the children would be the greatest tragedy."

"We just stay here?"

"Well," he hesitated. No, not yet. "For now, yes. The kittens aren't ready to travel yet. And the barn is a safe place for them."

"Why the barn?"

"My, might as well call it magic, is strongest out there, where I've worked the most. Sweated and bled and it's built on the remains of an even older structure, that was built by what you would call Native Americans. They weren't natives any more than we are, but it'll do for a quick naming. It had power when I found this place. So, the best place to keep the kittens hidden is there."

"Why are the kittens so important?"

She'd hit on it there. "I can't tell you that, either. Trust me they are, ok?"

"Well, I love my puddy paw babies, so I won't argue or ask too many questions. I do get OpSec, Grampa."

Heff laughed out loud at the seriousness of her combined with the baby talk and milspeak. "Good, then, you'll be my first soldier. But for now, first lesson."

Her face set in concentration immediately. "Yes, Grampa?"

"A soldier sleeps when he can, eats when he can. You never know when the next chance will come. So, you, princess, need to go to bed."

She wrinkled her nose at him, but left obediently. He watched her out to the barn and stood in the doorway watching the appearing stars and smoking his pipe for a very long time. He'd do anything to keep her safe - to keep them all safe - but he was beginning to fear it was too late for that. The stars here were so bright in the clear sky. He knocked the dottle out of his pipe and tipped his head back, looking up at the milky way. A dark shape swooped through his field of vision and he started, before realizing it was only a barn owl.

"Past time I was away," he muttered, reaching for his shearling jacket and shrugging it on. He wouldn't sleep tonight. He'd walk the land and reset wards. The babysitter would be here, soon, and Heff knew what he had to do, then.

5

SURVIVAL SKILLS

*I*n the morning, Linn milked the goats and fed the kittens, then her grandfather called her into the yard.

"Ever built a fire from scratch?" Heff asked. He stood there with his hands in his jeans pocket, looking relaxed and casual. Linn looked at him, puzzled. He was different today.

"I've made fires while out camping with Mom and Dad, they wanted to teach me how to take care of myself."

"Show me." He didn't move.

She looked at him for a minute and then realized he wouldn't help. She shrugged and trotted into the house. The things she wanted were easy to find. Back outside, she glanced around to pick a spot. Close by, there was really only one option. She knelt on the driveway and crumpled up paper, then grabbed some dead flower stalks from the border, and a few small pieces of kindling from the woodpile. She struck the match on the box she'd brought out, shielding it from the wind with her hand, and ignited the paper.

"Good. Do it again. House and woodpile off limits."

Heff dumped a bucket of water over her kindling blaze, and Linn hopped back, spluttering indignantly. He took the matches from her.

"But, but!"

"Nope. You can do it."

"I carry a match safe in the woods."

"How many matches in it?"

"Um, about a dozen?"

"What happens if you're out there," He indicated the looming mountains with a sweep of his arm. "More than a week?"

She sighed. She knew in theory how to do this. Looking grumpily back at him, she set off for the woods. This collection took a little longer. She was vaguely aware that Grampa Heff was in the woods nearby, but he was very quiet, and she didn't really want to talk to him, and wasn't about to ask for help.

The first thing she looked for was a paper birch. The bark was highly flammable and could be lit even wet. She had a handful of it in her survival kit, but Grampa had set the parameters, and her pack was indoors. All she had was her belt pouch and knife. This turned a difficult task into a time-consuming one. With her knife she cut dry twigs down and tied them into a neat bundle with braided grass and hung this from one of her belt loops. The birch bark went into her pocket along with a handful of dry grass. She found some dry, fallen wood. She didn't bother to break them, long pieces could be arranged radially and pushed in as they burned down.

When she walked out of the woods with her hands full, Heff was hunkered down by the long driveway. He nodded at her.

"Come t' house."

Linn followed him to the yard, where the fire ring he used for barbecuing had been cleaned out. He had a platter of food on the table. Linn laughed at that, and built the fire carefully. Bark first, shredded and cocooned with the dried grass. The twigs on that, then the tree limbs, arranged to give the kernel of the fire air. Pulling out her knife and flint striker, she rested the striker on the bark, pushing down firmly and creating a stream of sparks that jetted into the tinder. A couple of tries and she could see glowing spots that she blew on to feed the fire. Flames flicked up, and she rearranged the twigs to be in better contact with the tinder. Rocking back on her heels, she smiled up at her grandfather.

"Better?"

"Very good. I'll cook lunch while you check on the kittens."

Linn could feel her cheeks warm at his praise. Grampa Heff didn't do it much, and she knew she'd passed his first test. She wondered what the next one would be. The kittens were waiting for her at the gate, ready for their bottles. She felt guilty for having left them most of the morning, but then thought of a mother cat. The kittens would be alone while she was out hunting. Linn cuddled them and washed them after their bottles, until they were ready to fall asleep again. They slept a lot.

Her own stomach grumbled, and she sniffed. Grampa's cooking smelled good. She sniffed again. Smelled like bacon. Linn scrambled down the ladder and Grampa Heff handed her a plate full of bacon and eggs. He'd pulled and washed a handful of sorrel and lightly wilted it in the bacon grease. It was delicious, and she had seconds.

Her stomach full, she sighed and smiled up at him.

"Did I pass?"

"Yep. Figured your mom did ok with you. But I needed to be sure."

"We used to go camping a lot." Linn looked at the little fire dying into embers. Grampa had pulled it apart so it would go out. She felt happy. Her Dad would have liked what Grampa had done today. He'd taught her as much as her mother had. They had gone camping in all seasons, and she'd loved every trip.

"You miss him."

"Yeah, but it's ok. This... He would have liked this."

Heff nodded. "He was a good man."

"Did he know... about you, and Mom?"

Heff shook his head. "No, he didn't. But then, most mortals never know. We're safer that way, both mortal and immortal."

She nodded. "I won't tell."

"I know you won't. Now, I need to get some work done in the smithy today."

"I'll make dinner." She offered shyly.

Heff laughed. "I'll take you up on that, as long as it's one of your dad's recipes."

Linn laughed along with him, feeling something in her heart ease a little. If she couldn't have her father, she at least had the goodness that was her memories of him in her mind. Her mother really couldn't cook. Everything was burned or raw, with her. Linn had been her father's "little chef" since she could stand on a stool at his elbow, and she liked to cook. Tonight, she'd have fun.

"Well, if you're going to cook it, go out and get it." Grampa took her plate along with his.

"What?" Linn stared up at him in confusion.

"Kill it, clean it, and then cook it, girl. You won't always have a supermarket and a refrigerator at your beck and call."

"I don't know how." She protested.

"You shoot pretty good with your .22, your mom tells me."

"I didn't bring it."

"Well, here." Heff reached behind the woodpile and handed her a .22 rifle. Plain and worn, she could see immediately it was old.

"I've had it for a long spell. Time you got to take care of her."

He handed her a leather pouch which had six cartridges in it. "You can't get game with that many, we go hungry. Time will come you'll get two... one for each of us."

Linn nodded. She wasn't sure they wouldn't go hungry tonight. Her parents hadn't taught her how to hunt, or trap, although she'd read books about it.

Heff smiled. "Don't look so stricken. Go find a couple of rabbits, bring 'em home and I'll teach you how to clean them."

Linn put the pouch on her belt and picked up her day pack. She knew she needed to learn this, but this was challenging. Then she grinned. "All right, Grampa. I'll be home soon!"

Heff chuckled as she walked away. She was feisty. She had a chance in this messy world of theirs. He stretched a hand out over the fire, feeling the warmth of it, and then closed his fingers. The fire went out, and he could feel the energy he'd just absorbed racing through his body. Time to get to work.

6

SCHOLAR'S RECRUITMENT

Sekhmet licked a sore paw contemplatively. Even traveling the higher paths was hard on the feet when one had been gone as long as she had. Beast form made the travel easier to bear, but she was weary. No-one appreciates how large an entire planet really is until they try to visit a quarter of it within a month.

"At least it's not the whole damn thing." She snarled aloud. Her traveling companion looked at her in amusement.

"Dear lady, have strength. Vulcan will join us ere long and the fight will begin in earnest."

"You and your ye olde English. Shove it, Peter. My feet hurt. Battle comes and I'm going to be incapable of shifting a paw to help his generalship."

"The artificer will no doubt be surprised to hear his doughtiest warrior speak so." He intoned, but she could see the twinkle in his eye.

Sekhmet lifted her lips, baring her fangs. He just laughed and levered himself up with his staff. Unlike her, he was no immortal. His mortality was evident in his motions now as he stretched a little and began to walk. She paced alongside and he placed a hand on her withers, evidently grateful for the unspoken assistance. Here, in the higher plane, where time slipped by at a different rate, he was merely very old. Below in the human lands he would have been dust a century ago.

"Your children?" He asked after a few moments as his muscles loosened and he walked more easily. Sekhmet felt his weight taken from her.

"Are safe with the Guardian. She grows apace with them, Vulcan tells me."

"Good. The young ones should be spared." He sighed heavily.

"They never are." The big cat murmured in response to his unspoken memories of atrocities long past.

"The Scholar will give us some answers."

Sekhmet snorted. If the creature could be coaxed from its mad lair. Peter would help with that. He was often the only voice the Scholar heard in that cobwebby brain of hers. She believed he was an angel. Even Peter had stopped trying to persuade her otherwise.

Peter had come to the land above, which legends below named Fata Morgana, Atlantis, and dozens of other names, when he lay dying on a battlefield. The Scholar, known for her mad ways above and below alike, had come upon him, a broken human soldier. She had healed him and brought him here. He was by no means the only mortal here, although it had become very rare for humans to dwell in the higher plane in the last century.

Sekhmet sighed. She only vaguely remembered her mother's tales of the time before this plane had been created. When the creatures styled the Titans by the humans had burst through and fallen the long, long way to Earth. In the millennia since, these wars had erupted from time to time. It was like living on one of Vulcan's mountains of fire, she thought irritably.

The path twisted oddly, and then deposited them in the valley of twisted glass and stone that was the Scholar's home. Sekhmet sat down and curled her tail around her paws. This place gave her the creeps. Peter patted her on the head absently, then started forward, leaning on his cane. She looked after him affectionately. Even at this time of life, in what would be his eighties, she guessed, he was a striking figure. He looked back at her, his brilliant blue eyes flashing, and raised a hand in salute.

Once Peter was out of sight Sekhmet rose and began to pace across the valley, her tail lashing. Vulcan felt the Scholar would hold the key to their success, she knew. Secret weapon, indeed. She snorted.

The kittens would be ready soon to travel, and her last message from Vulcan had included that he intended to leave his charges with a babysitter when he came here to finish the organization of the effort. She snorted. It was going to have to be someone formidable to keep track of that girl, who she read as a person of great spirit and will, and her kittens. Sekhmet's last litter had been challenging. This was why she waited a few centuries between kittens.

A movement far up on the canyon wall caught her attention. With ears pricked forward, she slunk into a cluster of rocks, watching the area closely. She couldn't quite make out the shape of the intruder, which would be because he was using magic, she guessed. She waited in stillness, even her tail quiet for once.

She didn't stare at one spot, merely knowing where he was going, and kept scanning for other threats. There were approaching spots in the sky, too high even for her to see what they were, but she thought she knew. Peter and the Scholar would be no match for one of Zeus's thunderbolts.

Calmly she slid through the rocks, keeping to cover as much as she could. No point in drawing fire until she was in the Scholar's lair, which she was fairly sure had its own protections.

Under the first glassy arch, she broke into a lope. "Peter!" she roared.

Her voice echoed weirdly in there. The design of this place, with the glossy obsidian and rough sandstone, made her fur stand on end. The Scholar had died in fire once, and it had twisted her mind.

"Peter! Scholar! Run!" She roared again.

The two popped out of a side corridor. Sekhmet skidded to a halt, her claws throwing up sparks. She noted that absently as a cool effect.

"They're coming." She snarled.

The Scholar was wearing a knapsack and carrying a quarterstaff longer than she was with brass ferrules. Peter looked like he was breathless. Sekhmet growled and stretched. She could see Peter's eyes widen as she suddenly grew taller than a horse. Surely, he'd seen enough up here not to be startled at that little trick. She crouched and looked at him expectantly. Not every mortal could be granted what she was offering.

Peter scrambled onto her back, his lightness surprising her. The old man was... old, she thought fleetingly. Then she was running flat out, stretching with every stride for the entrance of the high path, where they would be sheltered from the deadly firebolts. The path was shielded. Peace bonded, Vulcan had once said.

The first trio of bolts struck the Lair while they were still short of the entrance, but had been aimed for the center. The Scholar cried out as if she were hit, but kept pace with Sekhmet, running faster than a human could have managed. Sekhmet knew the loss of her second home had to be hard, given how she'd reacted to the loss of the first one. Now wasn't the time, though.

They ran through the jumbles of rocks toward the path when the monster Sekhmet had watched climbing down the canyon was leaped out in front of them. She reached out a paw as she curved her body to the side, and felt her claws tear through the flesh of the Minotaur like paper. The Scholar on the other side spun her quarterstaff, bringing one end down on his head. He screamed and his knees buckled, then they were past.

Sekhmet felt her paws strike the slippery tough surface of the path, and the tips of her claws, still extended from excitement, bit into it. She stumbled, almost throwing Peter, then regained her footing. The Scholar was only a step behind and the path closed around them... then darkened as a firebolt made a direct hit on the end. She didn't even feel the overpressure.

Sekhmet didn't stop, but she did slow to a lope. She could feel the Scholar's hand on her shoulder, not pulling, but keeping contact. Good. She was going to ask the path for help and if they were all aligned it was easier. The Minotaur was behind them, still. He was mad. The Scholar wasn't right, but compared to the half-beast, she was delightfully eccentric. And Sekhmet might be immortal, but it still hurt to die.

She keened, pitching her voice to the frequency of the path. Her mother had taught her this while she was a kitten, and she'd used it rarely in times of great need. Hopefully she remembered the right notes. The path resonated around them, vibrating her to her bones like a great purr. Sekhmet sang the commands.

"Oh, I say, well done!" Peter spoke for the first time in his wild ride.

He went on in a resonant tone. "The Valkyrie's cry checks wild flight and guides us into night."

"*Not* a Valkyrie." Sekhmet told him when she could speak again. They were in night, though. She'd sung them to the far edge of the higher plane. She huffed out a great breath and dropped to a walk. The Scholar patted her shoulder. Sekhmet followed the woman's pointing finger and saw the glimmer of starshine on water. There was no moon here tonight, but the Milky Way stretched overhead brighter than it was in the human realm.

"Good idea." She stepped off the path, flexing her pads against the cool grass. Her feet started to hurt again. Funny how she never felt them when it was time to run. Peter slipped off her back and walked with her to the stream. The cool water tasted good. She lapped, and they lifted double handfuls to their mouths, all three of them keeping watches in different directions while they drank.

No movement broke the stillness of the night. Sekhmet opened her mouth and scented the air. There was a den of foxes upstream, birds in the trees, but no other warm bodies anywhere near. She sneezed and licked her nose. The dust from the Scholar's Lair still clung to it. She sneezed again, getting the last of it out.

"All quiet." She reported. "I think rest, and in the morning, I'll take the Scholar to Vulcan. If she stays on this plane she will be in danger."

She lay down, keeping her head up and alert. She could do without sleep. Peter needed it, and the Scholar might be an immortal, but Sekhmet always felt of her as a little old lady. The two leaned against her side and she could feel them relax as she began to purr.

In the morning, she would have to find a sanctuary for Peter. Returning to Earth would kill him, she suspected. The Scholar was going to have to come to Earth for the first time since her fiery death. That was going to be a scene.

Her ears flickered at a whisper of noise overhead, but even her great eyes couldn't pick out where the sound had come from. The stars gleamed down undimmed by the time passed since they had sent out their light. Sekhmet kept watch.

7

YOUNG HUNTRESS

*L*inn crouched in the noisy woods waiting for a rabbit to come hopping down the path. Who ever said woods were quiet, she thought crossly, must have been deaf. There were crows, over there, talking to each other in caws. A bold chickadee had been hopping from branch to branch over her head, scolding her anxiously, and a squirrel was chittering loudly across the trail. She knew if she stayed still long enough, they would lose interest, but in the meantime, dinner was no closer.

Her patience was rewarded by a flicker of movement she caught in the corner of her eye. A rabbit was on the edge of the glade, eating grass and looking up every so often, his big ears swiveling. Lin steadied the rifle on the branch and breathed slowly. He looked back down at the grass and she took her shot, squeezing gently. The rabbit leaped into the air and screamed, but when he hit the ground, he sprawled in a boneless heap. She waited a while anyway.

When she was quite sure he was dead and wouldn't jump up and run away she walked across the glade and picked him up. She'd made a clean head shot. He'd been dead before he hit the ground.

"Sorry, little guy." She murmured. Silly to talk to a dead animal, but it seemed right. "I need to learn. Thanks."

She put him into the plastic-lined game-bag Grampa Heff had given her so she wouldn't soil her daypack, and moved on to another likely spot. She only needed two for dinner. The quiet time in the woods was giving her time to think, too.

If Grampa and the other immortals were real, and they weren't magic, which is what Grampa had mentioned, what were they? Where did they come from? She's been reading origin myths of the gods. Many of them had the same theme, that of one generation of gods destroying another, and many referenced falling from one plane to another, trapping the gods here on Earth.

She also saw in the Orphic tales of the Titans the origins of the clash that was affecting her. The gypsum gods, the Olympians who had seized power, now wanted to claim the whole Earth. They saw the other families of gods, who had been revered by the Norse, the American Indians, and other peoples, as weak and inferior. This, combined with the rise of humanity and technology, threatened them.

Linn hunkered down on the little ravine overlooking the stream. Rabbits didn't look up much, she'd noticed. They should, hawks and eagles could take them. She glanced up herself, reflexively. Branches and leaves kept the sky from even being visible here.

It wasn't long before two rabbits appeared at the stream edge. When she shot one, the other took off like a streak of lightning. Linn stepped gingerly on rocks across the little stream, trying to keep her feet dry. Even in full summer, the mountain streams of Idaho weren't exactly balmy. She'd been in this one once before and it was icy all year round.

With two rabbits in the bag, she headed home, gathering a handful of sorrel at the edge of the trail as she walked. Chicken-fried rabbit, salad, and potatoes, she decided. Simple, but it'd be good. She was hungry already. Actually, she was hungry all the time. She knew it was because she was a teenager, but it didn't make her tummy rumble less. She pulled a bag of GORP out of her pack and munched.

The wild strawberries were gone by, but she knew where a patch of cloudberries was, and she knew how fond Grampa Heff was of them. She picked them every summer with her grandma for him. Linn sighed over the fragrant, tender golden clusters. She missed her grandmother's belly laugh, and the stories she told as they picked together. It wasn't as fun without a companion.

The she wondered who was coming to be babysitter. Would it be her grandmother? Who was her grandmother? Linn rocked back on her heels and looked up at the looming mountains. Her grandmother was a goddess, but Vulcan hadn't said which one. She wasn't an Olympian Linn was fairly sure. Her Gramma was too down-to-Earth. Linn chuckled at her inadvertent pun.

Time to go home and make dinner. Answers would come with time and patience in her experience. It had been years... five, at least, since she'd learned that staying quiet and out of sight meant she could hear adult conversations and learn all sorts of things. The babysitter should be here tomorrow.

She walked down the worn path from woods to house through the meadow relaxed and planning dinner in her head when the flames caught her attention. She was running through the grass toward them before she even thought about why the smithy would be burning. The barn wasn't alight, she saw quickly. Huge orange-red flames leaped and flickered up from the shop where Grampa Heff was working.

Linn didn't remember screaming, although later Heff told her she had been. Which is what brought him bursting out the doors toward her, through the flames and bringing them with him. Linn kept running toward him, seeing the fire on him, above him, all around the smithy... no smoke billowed up and she caught at his arms, shaking and not feeling any heat although she could see the flames. Her vision sparkled at the edges and she felt her knees give way and everything grayed out like a tunnel receding.

HEFF CARRIED his limp granddaughter into the house cradled into his arms. He didn't know what she had seen, but he'd seen the terror in her eyes as she'd collapsed at his feet. He laid her down on the couch and lifted her legs to lie on the arm of the couch, elevated over her heart. She opened her eyes but he knew she wasn't quite back yet.

"Shhh..." when she started to struggle, he leaned over her and pushed the hair out of her eyes. "Lie still. It's ok."

Her eyes closed again, then flew open a minute later.

"You're on fire!" she blurted.

He knew what was going on, now. "It's ok. Feel." He took one of her hands and placed it on his bare forearm. She flinched, then grabbed tightly.

"No heat, no fire. I'm all right."

She gasped and shuddered. "Thought you were burning." She managed finally.

Heff gathered her in his arms, forgetting that he was sweaty and covered in soot. "It is all right, child." She clung to his neck, eyes tightly shut. "You have the Sight. This is my blood coming to the fore in you. It's a common enough gift."

"Gift?" she choked. "I was so scared!"

"It will be a gift, once you're used to it and trained to use it."

He could feel her shaking ease. She still had her eyes closed. "What... what was I seeing?"

"Not the future, child. You are seeing my power."

She slowly opened her eyes, looking up at him. Her face relaxed. "I'm not seeing it now."

He nodded. "It will come and go at the beginning. You'll learn to use it, in time."

"So your... power... looks like fire."

"Yes. I'm the Smith, and god of Volcanoes, for a reason."

She sighed and buried her face in his shoulder for a minute. Then she sneezed. "A stinky one, too."

He laughed and let her sit up. "Why don't I go clean up while you prep for dinner. Feel like you can stand up now?"

He offered her and arm, but she was back to normal and as she stood up, realized she was still wearing the pack. "Oh, no! The berries!"

Heff laughed again as he went out the door with her laying things out on the table checking for damage. It had been a long time since life had felt this good. With the development of her power, the child's defenses were that much stronger. She made him laugh. He was going to miss her when he left tomorrow.

He stripped to the waist and washed in the cold water from the pump. Then he went into the forge and shut it down. Most of the power he pulled from the earth himself, but the fire was still essential to the metal work. He would come out here tonight and finish while she was sleeping, right now he felt the need to be near her, and he still needed to teach her to gut the rabbits.

Linn looked up as her grandfather walked back in the cabin, pulling a t shirt over his head. She raised an eyebrow at the worn Metallica design and muttered. "Figures."

"You need your knife, your kills, and to come out to the pump."

"Yes, sir." She grabbed the limp rabbits and followed him. She'd not taken the belt-knife off. She all but slept with it on, up here at Grampa's cabin.

"Normally, you will want to butcher immediately. You don't want to leave the carcass intact; it will spoil the meat."

She nodded. He picked up one by the hind legs.

"Cut the skin here and here." He sliced neatly around the rear hocks, and then from the inner leg all the way between them. "You'll be able to pull the skin down, like taking off a glove." He pulled the skin down the legs, then took hold and with one smooth motion inverted the skin completely. It looked like a white tube sock coming off, Linn thought.

"Cut the front feet off. Shears work well for this, too." He showed her, lying the carcass down in a stump and chopping them off quickly. Then he decapitated it. The hide went onto the woodpile, the feet and head into a nearby bucket.

"Your turn."

Linn quickly realized that it wasn't as easy as he made it look. Her hide had a couple little holes in it when she finally had it off. Rabbit skin was so thin. He showed her how to cut around the anus and slit carefully from tail to breastbone to remove the guts intact. Those went into the bucket as well, although he kept the thumb-sized hearts aside on the plate for the meat. She was slower than he, but managed not to puncture the gut and contaminate the meat. They washed the rabbits in the cold water and he took the hides and bucket of guts while she went inside with the carcasses to get dinner cooking.

By the time he came back indoors, she had the fat heated, the rabbits quartered and dredged in a flour mixture, and was cutting potatoes into French fries. She'd fry them along with the rabbit pieces. The salad was on the table already. He sat and filled a pipe quietly.

"Think any more about what happened?" He asked her.

"Not really." She kept her eyes on her work. The potatoes and sharp knife gave her a good excuse.

"You need to think about it, girl." he told her gently. "Need to be able to do that at will."

"Why?" she asked. It was bad enough to have other things in her life she couldn't control, like her emotions and hormones.

"Well, think about it. You're in a group of people and you need to know who's an immortal. Could be handy. And you can learn what wards are, and how to tell they are there, how to tell when someone's using power."

Linn nodded, laying the cut potatoes on paper towels to absorb the excess moisture.

"It has to be scary; I know. But once you learn to control it you'll be glad of it."

"How do I control it?"

"Hmmm. Look at me for a minute."

Linn laid the knife down and looked at him. No flames, just his gray hair disheveled from his last foray outdoors. He held out a hand and opened his fingers.

"Focus, that's it."

She stared at his hand. Ghostly flames seemed to dance in his palm. He closed his hand and they disappeared. She looked up at him and saw the flames in his eyes, they concealed his eyes and danced in the sockets... He blinked, and was just Grampa Heff again. "I saw..."

He nodded. "It will get easier. Don't burn dinner, now."

Linn thought all through dinner. Grampa seemed content to let her stew, barely speaking himself except to comment on dinner. They didn't eat all the fried rabbit, but as he commented, it would be good lunch the following day. He raised an eyebrow at the flowers in the salad, but ate them without comment.

8

MYSTERY BABYSITTER

*a*s Heff was washing up and she was wiping down the counters and stove, Linn finally asked the question she's been avoiding all day.

"Grampa, who is going to be babysitting?"

"It's not going to be your grandmother, girl. Sorry, but I need her where she is." He seemingly read her mind as she had been thinking about her grandmother earlier in the day.

"So, who?" She didn't look up; afraid he'd see the sudden tears in her eyes as he went on.

"You'll meet him tomorrow. He defies description, and the kittens are starving." Heff shooed her out of the house gruffly but gently. She guessed he knew how she was feeling.

Linn sighed and went out to the barn, where she found that Grampa had milked and filled bottles before dinner. That's what had taken him so long. The kittens were indeed convinced they were being starved, crying piteously at the gate for her.

She fed them, and cleaned the little pan. They were washing one another and her when it occurred to her to try the Sight on them. She squinted at each of them, but couldn't see anything other than little pink yawns and fuzz. Slightly disappointed, she curled up with the heap of kittens and drifted off to sleep to dream of floating down the Nile in a papyrus boat with the kittens, trying to steer clear of crocodiles and hippopotami.

She woke up to her watch alarm in the morning. Yawning, she climbed down the ladder and fetched the milk pail and Silly. She rested her head on the doe's warm flank and milked as she woke up. Milking was already an easy habit, as her muscles knew how to do it now. She headed into the house with the full milk pail, only to stop short at the sight of someone sitting on the front porch.

He was in Grampa's chair, with it tilted back around the wall, and his pipe wreathed smoke around his head. He was trying to look like Grampa Heff, but he wasn't. Linn squinted at him. Her Sight kicked in and she took a step back. The immortal on the porch was powerful. White light burst forth from him in waves, and she threw a hand up in front of her eyes to ward it off. She blinked furiously, trying to shut the Sight off again.

She heard the chair legs hit the wood. Steps came towards her and she closed her eyes tightly.

"You all right?" His deep voice was gruff but she could hear the concern.

"Yes - no... I'm still trying to figure out how to turn this on and off!" she burst out in frustration.

"Look at me..." He put a hand under her chin, warm fingers softly reassuring.

Reluctantly, Linn opened her eyes. Sighing with relief, she realized she could see again. She was looking straight into the eyes of a very short black man, who was grinning at her. His hair and goatee were snow white, but he didn't look old.

"You're the babysitter?" She blurted.

He let go of her chin and took a step back, then swept her a flourishing bow.

"At your service, Linnaea. I am Bes. Sometimes known as a god, although I prefer... cosmic clown." He cut a caper. She laughed in surprise.

"Don't spill the milk, child." He was back to being serious now. "Come in, you've passed the first test."

"Which was?" she asked warily, following him up the porch steps.

"To see through the illusion, of course. And I was laying it on thick, being forewarned that you had seen through Mars' sleep spell."

"Which was why you almost blinded me with the power." She said ruefully.

"True. But you did see it truly before the Sight kicked in. You really will have to learn to control that."

"Grampa keeps telling me that."

"Keeps telling you what?" Her grandfather's voice came from in the house. Linn headed for the sink with the milk pail.

"I need to control my gift."

"I see you met Bes." His suppressed laughter warmed his voice.

Linn glared at them both over her shoulder, then turned back to her task, hearing Bes' delighted chuckle behind her.

"Feisty, isn't she. She'll do, Heff."

Linn blushed as she heard that. Her grandfather laughed. "You'll have your hands full with this lot, I'm afraid. The kittens are about ready to leave the barn."

"And the girl?" Bes and her grandfather walked out onto the porch. The last thing Linn heard was her grandfather's voice.

"Teach her to be sneaky..."

She sighed. Her babysitter was a clown. Evidently a sneaky one, but still! She put the milk pail to dry and walked over to the bookshelf. She found Bes in the Standard Dictionary of Folklore. He was an Egyptian god, she read, known for his protection of children and pregnant women. His other aspect was the god of war and vengeance. She slid the book back in its place. It figured Grampa would choose him, then. He has all the right characteristics, she thought, to protect us, and to teach me.

The door opened, and she turned to see Bes and her grandfather come in. Her grandfather was carrying a cloth-wrapped bundle. He set it down on the table and Linn dried her hands and walked over to him. He wrapped her in his arms, holding her tightly enough that she squeaked.

She felt his chest rise and fall with an unheard sigh. "I hate to leave you, girl."

She looked up at him. "Go do what you need to. Just like I told Mom." Linn frowned. "Is she safe, by the way?"

"Linn, your mother really is a goddess." Bes interjected. "She is a formidable one, too." He looked thoughtful. Linn wondered what the story was, there, and made a mental note to pry it out of him sometime.

Heff smiled at her. "Your mother is currently traveling around the world to volcanoes and calderas like the one under Yellowstone. She's tapping and controlling energy to keep them from all erupting as the Olympians draw power from the Earth's core."

Linn gaped at him. "Draw power from the core?" she managed. "But..."

"I've told you enough for now. Your mother's work is crucial to keeping this world's ecosystem viable. That weapon was used once before, I won't let that happen again." He looked grim, and Linn remembered her promise about OpSec.

"Yes, Grampa." She responded quietly.

"Now," he let go of her and stepped back. "I have a present for you. Close your eyes, and hold out both of your hands."

Linn held them out obediently, palms up and closed her eyes. She felt Grampa put something cool and heavy in them, and then his big, warm hands closed over hers. He was murmuring something, but she couldn't hear the words. Then Bes was speaking, too, and touching her forearms. Linn felt a flash of heat travel through her.

She gasped and opened her eyes. The Sight flickered and she saw a flare of power from both men, extended from them to the sword in her hands. Her eyes widened. They stepped back and she was left holding onto it, still glowing slightly. It was warm now, she realized.

"She is bonded to you." Grampa Heff told her quietly. "Your weapon. There is enough power in it to injure even a god. Carry her always. Sleep with her, even. You understand?"

Linn nodded, speechless. She was scared, and excited. A tumble of emotions flooded through her. Her grandfather looked as grim as she had ever seen him. She opened her mouth, and then shut it again, unsure what to say.

Bes broke the silence. "Sure, and she needs a name."

Linn looked at the leaf-bladed sword blankly. She recognized the style from swords Grampa had made in the past. The smaller size would make it possible for her to wield. A two-handed broadsword like you saw in movies would have been ridiculous for her. Power still flickered along the edges of the blade.

"She is Lambent." The voice wasn't hers, although it came from her mouth. Linn felt funny, and swayed as she stood. Grampa stepped quickly to her side and took Lambent from her hands, sliding an arm around her shoulders. Linn staggered and felt her vision graying out again.

"Not again!" she cried as her knees went out from under her. This time, she was glad to hear, it was her own voice. Bes caught her. She couldn't move, but could still see and hear as he carried her to the couch with surprising ease for someone shorter than she by a full inch.

She could hear them talking as they stood over her. Lambent was on the table. Linn was aware of where the sword was, like it was part of her body. She lost track of reality for a minute, and stood in a swirling, misty grayness. Fog, damp on her skin. Lambent was in her hand, and a softly-furred skull was pressed into the palm of the other hand. She raised Lambent, glowing like a torch, and screamed hoarsely as the kitten... Blackie, she realized... roared his defiance with her. Then she was lying on the couch in Grampa's living room, gasping for breath and crying out.

Grampa Heff was holding her. "Shhh... it's all right. You're ok. Relax. Let it go."

Linn shuddered and leaned back on the couch. She still couldn't move. Bes lifted her legs onto the arm like Grampa had done before. She felt the blood coming back to her brain. "You feeling better?" Grampa asked. She nodded, afraid to speak again. "All right. Just rest a bit."

Both of them went onto the porch, leaving the door open so they could check on her, she guessed. Her head was swimming, and after one attempt to sit up she let that go until later. She could hear them talking, although they were trying to keep their voices down.

"Same thing as happened with the first Sight?"

"Yes, she fainted then, too."

"She's developing fast. Sight, now Foresight."

Grampa Heff huffed out a short breath. "It worries me more that with each manifestation she does this. It makes her vulnerable."

"I have her back, Heff. You have to go."

"You have her back? You are her Protector!" Her grandfather protested.

"Lower your voice, Heff." Linn heard a touch of humor in Bes' voice. "Yes, her back. I let few know how much of the Second Sight I have. You know where I come from."

"You're one of the oldest."

"So I am. Which may explain my madness."

Heff laughed. Bes continued, his voice deep and quiet. Linn felt it ripple through her like a pebble thrown in a pond. "Linnaea, go to sleep, child."

Linn felt her mind's eyes close, and she sighed as sleep took her. She felt a slight sense of indignation that he'd put her to sleep and out of being able to eavesdrop.

She was vaguely aware that her grandfather was leaning over her. She opened her eyes, and he smiled at her and kissed her forehead. Then her eyes were so heavy and she closed them again.

She awakened to Bes shaking her shoulder. He grinned down at her. "Going to sleep all day?"

"Um..." Linn rubbed her eyes. They felt like glue had been poured into them. "Grampa?"

"Has gone. It's time for you to start training."

"What? He left?" She felt all muzzy. "Training?"

"Seems you have a sword to learn how to use. Can't chop off your own toes." He commented dryly.

She sat up. It was, by the sun in the window, a couple hours later than it had been. She glared at him. "What did you do to me?"

"You took a little nap."

"I did not. You put me to sleep." Linn was furious.

"Well, and if I did..." He grinned again. "I can do it again when you're being annoying."

9

THE LIBRARIAN

Sekhmet, still in great cat form, sat Sphinx-like watching the scene play out with wry amusement. They had returned to the high path after a restless night and traveled to the court of Quetzalcoatl. Now that rainbow-feathered personage sat on his throne perch and hissed in frustration. Facing him were the Scholar and Peter, a strange pair in that blazoned room of great stone blocks and barbaric grandeur.

"Scholar. You must leave the high Plane and return to Earth. You are unsafe here." He insisted.

"I won't. They ruined my home!" she wailed, her hands fluttering. Abruptly, she realized what she was doing and crossed her arms across her chest and glared at the Mayan god. He sighed and rattled his feathers.

"You will. You are needed below in the battle against the Olympians." He still sounded firm, but he had gentled his voice for her.

"What can I offer?" she snapped back.

"You know more about the Old Ones' nature than anyone else in either plane. We need that knowledge if we are to foil their plans." He was practicing patience, but she was trying it.

"Foil their plans? Really, you just said that?" She was a past mistress of sarcasm, too.

Sekhmet suppressed a chuckle. The Scholar never pulled her punches, even with a senior immortal. The feathered serpent directed a fiery green eye in her direction and she looked back calmly. She could, of course, just scoop the Scholar up and take her willy nilly, but it would be better if the irascible demi-god was persuaded to go on her own.

Peter interjected. "Hypatia, dear. You really should consider it. Humans have grown so much in the time you were gone."

She looked at him, and Sekhmet saw the tears on her cheeks.

"I... don't want to leave you." The old woman looked at the old man mournfully.

Their love was a strange one, the demi-goddess crippled by the burning of her library and the English soldier left to die in the blistering sun so far from the green hills of home. The gods knew they had seen stranger ones. Now he held out his hand to her. She uncrossed her arms and took it in both of hers.

"I will be here when you get back. It will be a grand adventure, old girl."

Hypatia sniffled a little. Then she looked back at Sekhmet.

"Will I have access to a library?"

"Scholar, have you heard of the internet?"

The scarred old woman shook her head. Sekhmet broke into a very un-cat like grin. "Oh, this is going to be fun!" she chortled.

"Where are we going?" Hypatia looked interested now, not just combative.

"A very safe place. I think you will like it. There are sandy beaches and palm trees."

The Scholar snorted at the idea of a vacation spot. "I'll do fine in a nice room full of books, thank you."

"You can have your books on the beach." Sekhmet assured her with a laugh.

Peter and the serpent god watched the women walk out of the room together. The last thing they heard was Sekhmet's rumbling murmur repeating. "Oh, this is going to be fun..."

The god and the mortal looked at one another. Quetzalcoatl sighed. "Her sense of humor is irrepressible, isn't it?"

"The most charming thing about her. That, and those long claws protecting my heart from harm."

The serpent nodded knowingly. It had to be hard on the old soldier to not be able to accompany Hypatia. "What are your plans, Peter?"

He shrugged. "I hadn't any, really. Waiting... the lot of the tommy from time immemorial, eh?"

"I rather think we can put that mind of yours to work, old friend." The Serpent slithered off his throne. "Come with me, please?"

"Gladly, old chap. I rather fancy your idea."

10

TRAINING

*L*inn wasn't having fun. In the two days since Grampa had left, Bes had barely let her rest, let alone sleep. He'd been drilling her with Lambie for hours each day, and then running her ragged through the woods. The only good thing was that the kittens were now in the house.

When she had slept the night before, it had been in an exhausted heap with them all on the couch. Lambent, sheathed and in the crook of her arm, had glowed when all the kittens curled up with her. Linn had fallen asleep staring at the flickering power dancing above them.

Linn awakened to find Bes standing over her with a ferocious frown on his face and a kitten climbing his leg. He peeled Spot One off and handed him to Linn.

"Feeding time, girl. Time for them to learn how to lap from a bowl."

Linn untangled herself awkwardly from the sword and a couple of kittens. Blackie was staggering determinedly across the floor toward the table where the milk pail was. At six weeks old they could get around well enough, but the smooth floors in the cabin were a change from the hay in the loft. The big kitten... as big as a full-grown housecat already... kept losing his footing.

Linn set Spot one down on the floor and belted Lambent on, before looking for a stable bowl they wouldn't knock over. She finally dug two flat bottomed stoneware casseroles out of the cupboard. Bes, sitting in a kitchen chair playing with Spot Two, didn't say anything, but Linn saw one corner of his mouth quirk up.

She ignored him. Pouring the milk into the two bowls, she sat on the floor with them in front of her. The kittens came to her when she called, and she dipped her fingers in the milk and offered it to them. Giggling as they licked her fingers, she coaxed the kittens to put their noses into the milk. Patches inhaled some, and backed up, sneezing. Blackie plunged in and came up spluttering. Seconds later her was in the bowl, front paws and all, slurping noisily. The Spots followed his example and dove in the same bowl. Linn pulled Spot One out and put him by the other bowl, then tried to get Patches back in the game.

By the time they all had full, round little bellies, the floor was covered in milk, as was Linn. She scooped the roaming kittens up and put them on the couch, where they lined up and watched her as she mopped the floor. She put away the mop and went out to find Bes. The kittens crashed on the couch, asleep already.

Bes had left her a note tacked to the barn door.

"Chickie," it read. "Gone to pick up something. Stay in the wards. Enjoy your morning off."

Linn looked at the driveway. She hadn't even heard him pull out. How was he able to snooker her when Mars hadn't been? She knew what she needed to do with this unexpected time. She went back into the house, stopping to pat Blackie's silky head. Since the dream, vision, whatever it was, she felt a special bond with the biggest kitten. He stretched, slitting open his eyes and then licking her hand roughly. He was asleep again almost instantly.

Linn pulled an armload of books off the shelves and spread them out on the table. She couldn't sit on the couch; it was full of kittens. But she needed to know more about her enemies. She had read some of the modern re-tellings of the myths, most of which were ludicrous compared to the original legends. The originals were so dark, she realized, leafing through a very old translation from ancient Greek tales. Full of blood, pain and death... Linn shivered as she read. She could see that her grandfather had scribbled notes in the margins, but the ink was faded brown with time. He'd probably bought this book new, she thought.

It made her reflect again on the age of her grandfather. And Bes, she now thought, was older even than Vulcan. Bes was, from the accounts she'd read, one of the originals that had fallen from the other plane, whatever that was. Wherever that was, she corrected herself thoughtfully.

11

INTRODUCING THE LIBRARY

Sekhmet brought the Scholar to earth gently, avoiding cities and humans in general. The immortal's grasp on reality was tenuous at best, and the great cat wanted to keep her functional. Her last death had been a bad one, and while an immortal couldn't die permanently, the scarring on her face was a symbol of the scars to her soul. An immortal didn't need to wear scars, deformities, or wounds. As long as they had the energy, they could heal themselves, and others, as the Scholar had done with Peter.

For now, they paced through a wet forest, the rain falling unheeded as the Scholar touched leaves and flowers with delight. Sekhmet switched her tail slowly as they walked, impatient to be on, but unwilling to break the delight the Scholar showed with the verdant beauty around them. Her paws sank into the wet leaves deeply, where the Scholar, she noted with amusement, left no tracks at all. Her power was causing the immortal who chose to look like a little old lady to float, never touching the ground.

They came out of the jungle abruptly, to a cliff over-hanging the ocean. the Scholar clutched at Sekhmet's shoulder.

"Oh, my..." she gasped. "How beautiful. And it just goes on and on."

Sekhmet slitted her eyes against the bright sun glinting off the brilliant blue ocean and sniffed at the sea breeze that gently flirted with her fur.

No one was near that she could smell upwind. Time to take the Scholar to her library and leave all this pleasantness behind. She sighed.

"Follow me carefully." she told the old woman. The path was all but invisible from above, merely a jagged crack in the cliff edge. Sekhmet stepped carefully onto it, feeling her claws extend slightly as the sea was directly beneath her, crashing waves breaking on jagged lava flow. The path was well worn, for all the secrecy. Bare human feet had been treading it for centuries. Behind her, the Scholar followed unhesitatingly.

The path dipped into the cliff wall, through a narrow cleft that brushed both of Sekhmet's shoulders. Just as she was considering shifting forms to her slenderer human shape, it widened and she was standing in an almost perfectly tubular tunnel. Lights hung from the ceiling, lighting the glassy black walls. The Scholar touched the wall and muttered.

"Yes?" Sekhmet asked, unsure if she had been addressed.

"An old lava tube. Remarkable." the woman exclaimed.

"Your hostess thought it would be a secure location for your library and lab." Sekhmet told her.

"So, we are close, then."

"Yes, follow me." The big cat was careful not to move too quickly, although she was sure Hypatia could keep up. No point in pushing the Scholar, she would just push back.

Sekhmet paced off a quarter of a mile as the humans counted it, before she they came to a round wall blocking the tunnel. An ordinary steel door was mounted in it, with an iris scanner at the lock. Sekhmet looked into that, wincing as she was scanned. Cat's eyes were too sensitive for these things.

She could hear the click as the door unlocked, and the Scholar pulled it open for her. Handles were awkward with paws. She could shift to human form, but with all the tension staying a great cat was far more comfortable. She felt safer in this form. The look of the tunnel changed immediately. No longer bare walls of lava, they were now painted and there was a linoleum floor. They came to a second door, this one a simple wooden door, and it swung open with a push of Sekhmet's nose. She held the door open for the Scholar with one paw.

"Enter, lady." the cat bade her companion with a hint of a purr in her voice.

"Ah…" the Scholar sighed as she stepped into the great chamber. Lined with shelves of books from floor to the distant ceiling, the stacks radiated out from the center of the vast room, where a circular table stood, surrounded by chairs. A couple of ratty couches were arranged near it in a comfortable seating arrangement. Sekhmet know from experience it was a great place to study with a group. Or to play games.

The Scholar seemed to straighten and grow as she walked to the nearest shelf. Sekhmet sat, curled her tail around her paws and purred. The lights brightened a little. Sekhmet glanced up ruefully at the ornate chandeliers and toned it down a little. Last time she'd blown bulbs here the librarian had made her change them. That had not been a pleasant chore.

The Scholar turned back to the cat; her eyes bright. "This is a well-appointed library, indeed."

"Good. Let me show you to your chambers, then, and you may return here afterwards."

They paced slowly through the library, as the Scholar stopped every so often to exclaim over a volume she'd spotted. Sekhmet ruefully thought of the human phrase 'herding cats' and tried to keep the woman moving forward. Finally, at the outer ring of the library, which was shaped like an eye when viewed from above, they met some of the librarians.

Sekhmet bowed to the tiny persons who stood waiting for them. Paws together, she lowered her body, and almost brushed the floor with her nose. Hypatia picked up her cue and sank into the human version of a courtesy.

The coblyns were a chancy people. They had lurked in Welsh mines for centuries before beginning a slow diaspora across the globe, and they were the original goblins. Treated with respect they were happy and helpful. Slighted, their anger could be terrible. The band that watched over the library was probably the most easy-going she had ever met, but it never hurt to be careful of a proud people.

"Aloha!" the tallest coblyn called as they reached them. He stepped forward, lei in hands. Sekhmet crouched to allow him to put it around her neck, reducing her size as he did. One of the others did the same for the Scholar, who actually blushed and patted the lush flowers she had been given. Sekhmet eyed her with amazement. The years were literally falling away from the Scholar.

"Hail, Hypatia, mother of libraries. My name is Dafydd, these are Llewelyn and Lily." The other coblyns dipped bows to the Scholar, who was beaming at them, obviously enchanted with the little ceremony. "These ladies are at your service for research assistance, and in any other needs you may have. If you will follow us?" He gestured toward the massive double doors that led out of the library, and then began walking, assuming they would follow.

Sekhmet smiled at the byplay. They ought to have done this years ago, instead of allowing the Scholar to retreat so far away from the human realm. Forgotten, she padded at the back of the little entourage, listening to the conversation that was mostly about books. She felt a touch at her shoulder and looked into the face of their hostess.

Letting the others go ahead out of sight, she looked into Pele's eyes. The goddess was in Crone form, leaning on an ebonywood staff. The flames leaped in her eyes. Sekhmet was undisturbed by the immortal's fierce expression.

"The pieces draw together, Pele. All was well last time I saw them." She answered the unspoken questions."

"Good. And the little ones?" The concern in her voice softened the fierceness.

Sekhmet chuckled. "Not so little. They grow fast."

"I cannot leave here, you know." She whose power was so woven into the soil and seas of this place that the very ground glowed when seen with the Sight, and who had been a terrible enemy to those who invaded, laid a tremulous hand on Sekhmet's shoulder. Sekhmet licked Pele's cheek. She understood the old woman's dilemma. Torn between duty and family. Pele laughed, a rusty sound.

"You are a most impertinent cat."

"I am that." Sekhmet agreed contentedly.

"Keep an eye on him." The little tremble was back.

"As always. Bes is with the little ones, now. Vulcan goes to

Quetzalcoatl's court. I will join him there, now that the Scholar is safely with you."

Pele nodded. "Blessings on your journey." she intoned, touching the cat softly on the forehead. Power flickered on her fingertips, and Sekhmet felt the burn as the goddess gave her energy. She stretched her head out and bumped her nose against Pele's, evoking another laugh from the goddess whose wrinkles were only temporary, fitting her awful mood. Then the big cat turned and loped back the way she had come. Time to join the battle.

1 2

CATCHING A RIDE

*L*inn was still sitting at the table, making notes in a lined pad she'd found on the bookshelf, when Bes called her to come outside. Again, she hadn't heard him until he wanted her to. Annoyed with this failure on her part, she went out onto the porch and felt her irritation dissolve away.

"Oh! They are so beautiful..." She walked down to where he stood holding the reins of the two most beautiful horses that she had ever seen. One was a buckskin, the other a palomino, but both sported the classic white spotted blankets of an appaloosa. Bes grinned. He held the reins of the palomino out to her.

"Can you ride?"

"A little."

"She's well broken. You'll do fine, she'll take care of you."

Linn looked at him, then at the horse. She focused and her Sight kicked in. She staggered a little, then when Bes caught her elbow, she straightened. His aura was flaming white, still too bright to look at directly. The horses, though... Little flickers of green, green as grass, danced over them. The mare pricked her ears at Linn and blew a little, relaxing into a hip-shot pose, obviously bored.

"Bes, are they...?"

He let go of her and she closed her eyes, trying to turn the Sight back off. "No," she heard him say. "Merely warded with the power of their owner. Good, child, you're seeing better."

Linn opened her eyes and was relieved to be able to see normally again. "Who is their owner? Do all immortals have different colors? What kind of horse are they?"

Bess threw up a hand, laughing, to ward off her questions. "I'll answer as we go. I'd like to be back before the kittens awaken."

Linn nodded and put her foot in the stirrup. She swung up awkwardly. She only rode in the summer when visiting Grampa Heff, so she was out of practice. She settled into the deep-cantled saddle, liking the way it held her legs in place. A roping saddle, she wouldn't fall out of this easily. She looked over at Bes, who looked very much at home atop the gelding. The dwarf god ought to have looked absurd, but he didn't, just relaxed and confident.

"Where are we going?" she asked him.

"I need to show you the wards and teach you how to make them yourself." He nudged the gelding with his heels and the horse ambled to a start.

Linn felt her eyes widen a little. She couldn't do wards; she didn't have the power like they did. Bes headed toward the woods. She let her mare come up alongside him, where she could talk easily to him while they still covered open ground.

"So, who did you borrow the horses from?"

"Coyote, of course. Old dude packs serious mojo, and I had to talk to him anyway."

Linn blinked, trying to wrap her mind around the Egyptian god's words. He'd talked to the creator god of Native American legend? She tried to remember what she had read about that entity. "Um... isn't he another trickster god?"

Bes chortled. "Yes, indeed he is. Maybe the trickiest of us all."

"Do you know Loki?" Linn asked him next.

"You ask a lot of questions, anyone ever tell you that?" He grinned toothily at her.

"Frequently." She responded drily.

Bes went off into gales of laughter, clutching the saddle horn. Linn regarded him with mild irritation. He annoyed her more than anyone she could remember meeting, but she still liked him.

Finally, he straightened and wiped his eyes. "You remind me so much of your grandfather. Yes, I knew Loki."

"Knew?" Linn thought the immortals couldn't be killed.

"Long story. Catch me some winter night and I'll tell you, child."

They entered the forest, and Linn reined her mare back until she was behind him. They fell into silence, both of them aware of the forest and not needing to speak. Bes pointed and then veered off the path. Linn stayed with him, weaving through the trees in the open forest here. There was little brush, and she enjoyed the spicy scent of the forest as they traveled further than she had been before.

Bes stopped the gelding in a little glade with a cairn of rocks in the center of it. He pointed to that. "Look at that with your Sight, child."

Linn focused on it, and watched as it began to blaze with the orange-red she associated with her grandfather already. A thin thread of light stretched off in either direction. Bes dismounted and put his hands on the top rock in the pile. He closed his eyes and Linn could see the power flowing from him and mixing with the power her grandfather had left there. The flames leapt up and the thread got thicker.

Bes looked around at her, his eyes flickering with the power. "Come down, child."

Linn slid off her horse and joined him by the uncanny fire.

"You asked if every immortal had a different color. Not quite, but there are some who say they can tell whose power is whose by the shades."

He took her hands in his and held them to the cool, rough surface of the rock. She could feel the warmth of his Power flowing through her skin. It prickled a little. She watched the flickering light dance through both their skin with fascination. Then she could see filaments of fuchsia join his white. She jerked her hands away with a cry.

"Was that me?"

She was wringing her hands together as she backed away. They tingled painfully.

"Yes. Your Power, not much, but enough that anyone trying to enter the wards would alert you." He answered her question quietly.

Linn shook her hands and blew on them. "It hurts!" She scolded him.

He nodded. "It's not an easy thing to use. Your grandfather and I have been doing it for so long... well, I feel it, I'm not sure he still does."

"Why didn't you warn me?" Linn demanded.

"Didn't want to scare you, and I was helping."

Then the other thing registered. "Pink?! My power is pink?"

He laughed. Linn glared at him.

"I... don't... like... pink!" She hissed, and then mounted up again.

Bes again got in the saddle much more gracefully than someone who looked as old as he did ought to be able to manage.

"Why do you and Grampa even bother looking old?" She asked. He looked at her and she felt her face flush. She was being rude. "Sorry." She mumbled, looking down at her mare's mane.

"What?" He prompted, pretending to have not heard her.

Bes reined his gelding closer.

Linn repeated, louder "Sorry." and gave him a look.

"I can't give you all the answers today. Or even in a year. Some things you might never know. But this one's easy. How do you think humans would react to people living amongst them that never aged?"

He rode off and she followed him silently, thinking about that. He was right. Historically people had been pretty brutal to outsiders. How many lifetimes had the immortals chosen to live, pretending to die and then reappearing somewhere else, far from family and home?

She maneuvered up alongside him and reached over to put a hand on his sleeve.

"Bes, I'm sorry. It's all just... so much."

"Sometimes I forget just how young you are. Child, it's a long life you've got, never mind what me and your Grampa got to put up with. Now, we have five more wards to get to."

She fell back again silently. He helped with the other wards but by the time they were done with the last one she could feel tears rolling down her cheeks. Her hands hurt so badly she could barely move her fingers.

"Home and dinner will mend much of it." Bes told her gruffly, handing her a red bandana to wipe her face with.

Linn just nodded. She was so tired he had to help her remount, and she just followed him home, reins lying slack on the mare's neck. The mare was happy to follow her brother the gelding, so Linn just let her mind go blank. When they got back to the cabin, she was half-asleep on the horse and she slid off into Bes' arms. He carried her to the couch like a baby, shooing kittens who met them at the door.

Linn settled into the soft cushions and sighed. Blackie leapt up on her chest and licked her face. She giggled and touched his nose. A spark of pink flew out and he jerked his head back. For a moment she was afraid she'd hurt him, but then he butted her hand with his head and began to purr.

Patches climbed up on the back of the couch and joined in the purring. Lin reached up and stroked her too, the soft fur feeling good on her sore hands. Bes was ladling stew into bowls. They had left the pot on the banked wood stove all day. He brought the bowl to Linn and lifted Blackie down when he showed interest in the venison stew.

"They'll be eating solid food in a week. Two weeks and they can travel."

Linn wondered where they were going, but she was too tired to ask questions right now. The stew smelled wonderful, and tasted just as good. She inhaled her bowl full, and got up to refill it. Bes was sitting at the table with the kittens at his feet drinking their milk. She joined him, feeling much better.

"There you go, color back in your cheeks. Power takes a lot out of you. You won't be able to do this often, and when you do, lots of fuel."

Linn nodded. She was finally filling up and starting to feel sleepy. Bes motioned her away when she got up to do the dishes. "Not tonight. Get some sleep. Go purr on her, Blackie." He pointed at the couch and Linn went. For a wonder, so did Blackie, who reassumed his spot on her chest. He was really too heavy to do that for long, so she rolled onto her side and tucked him along her arm. He complied, and then she felt Spot One jump up and curl up in the crook of her knees.

Linn was asleep before the others joined them. She dreamed of the fog again, but this time she had Lambent in her sheath, so there was no light. She was walking on and on, so tired... she tripped over something soft and fell down, down...

She sat up with a start. She was still on the couch. Lambent was on the table where she had left her after dinner. The kittens were all over her and the couch. Blackie yawned until she could see the moonlight glinting on his little fangs. He put a firm paw on her chest and she laid back down. This time she didn't dream.

13

STORM CLOUDS GATHER

In the morning Linn milked the goats, barely noticing Lambent at her side. Working with the sword constantly with her had been annoying at first, but now she was used to it. Bes wandered out, a cup of coffee in hand, and tossed hay to the horses who were in the corral off the side of the barn.

"I want to get the kittens outside for a bit today. Sunny and warm." He leaned over the gate and watched her milk for a moment.

Linn nodded and wondered if she could get away with a cup of that coffee. She left the door propped open when she went inside and the kittens all tumbled over to stand and sniff excitedly, but none of them stepped outside. She put down their milk and they scrambled back to eat, making her laugh. She poured a cup of coffee and added fresh milk and spoonfuls of sugar. It still didn't taste great, but she sipped at it.

Bes walked up onto the porch. "Come on, then." He prompted.

Linn walked outside and Blackie followed on her heels, tail straight in the air. His ears, too big for his body, swiveled at every sound. Linn commented, "He has his mother's ears."

Patches and Spot Two hung in the doorway. Linn wondered if them being girls had anything to do with their hesitance. Spot One ventured to the top of the steps and wobbled on the edge. Linn scooped him up and rubbed her face on his side. The kittens were still so soft, but already bigger than a full-grown housecat. He wriggled to get down and she put him back on the porch. He lashed his tail and pounced on a leaf.

Blackie prowled over the whole porch, bouncing sideways once in a while at things Linn couldn't see. The girls finally ventured out, and Linn sat down to pat them and rub their ears. Patches climbed into her lap and watched the world from this sanctuary. Spot Two joined her twin in exploring.

Bes let Blackie climb his leg and took the big kitten into his arms. Linn winced, watching them. "Doesn't that hurt?"

"A little, but he's surprisingly careful for a kitten."

"They all are. I remember my cousin's cat had kittens a couple years ago and they scratched us all up, but they didn't mean to."

Blackie turned his head back and forth as they were talking, as if he were listening. Bes ran his fingers under the kitten's jawline, starting him purring.

"This might be the last peaceful day we have for a while, Child."

Linn bit her lip. "You said we were moving."

He nodded. "The wards here are strong, and attuned to all of us, now. But there is a lot of open ground, and Coyote has decided to join Heff. Without him here in the mountains, watching..." He shrugged and put Blackie down again. The kitten promptly pounced on Spot Two and rolled his sister across the weathered boards.

"Why us. I mean... you're pretty powerful. But the kittens, and me, well, we are hardly a threat."

"The kittens are full immortals. Children of Sekhmet, the Egyptian goddess of war and vengeance. And the Mayan god of Terrestrial Fire, which means that like your grandfather they are attuned to volcanoes. Something I don't think anyone has told you, is that we immortals don't have children often. For one thing, it takes a lot of Power to generate a viable pregnancy. For another, the untrained immortal child is a danger to himself and others." He suddenly looked as old as his grey hair made him out to be. She guessed he was remembering. Her grandparents had gotten that look from time to time, and it was only now she was understanding it.

"Terrible things, child, have come from that. And because a full immortal cannot be killed... we do have prisons, you know."

She nodded. "I'd guessed that from reading the myths and legends. Even a god can be locked away with enough power."

He nodded. "I myself have raised children. Over the ages I have become the one chosen to watch many children grow and guide them. Which is how I became the patron god of childbirth and children." He grinned suddenly. "Really ought to be a woman's job."

Linn laughed. "I'd wondered about that. Who are your adopted children?"

"Bast is one. The other... did not stay among mortals."

Linn looked down at Patches, now napping in her lap. "I am sorry."

"It has been many millennia. Some days, I forget."

The other kittens were stretched out in the sun. Blackie was washing his paw, which Linn had noticed was getting huge. Bes looked down at him.

"He's all paws and ears." The old god said affectionately.

Linn giggled. "I hope he grows into them."

She looked up at Bes, an odd feeling since they were usually nose to nose. "What are we doing today?"

"First, get this lot tucked in on the couch."

Linn nodded, scooping up Patches. She suspected Bes was enhancing the kitten's nap time to give them time for her lessons. As long as the kittens were safe. Once all the sleepy babies were poured onto the couch, she rejoined Bes on the porch in the warm sunlight, leaving the door closed behind her.

"How much tracking do you know?"

"I know what made what tracks, usually..."

"So, not a lot." His chuckle took the sting out of that. "Let's start with something easy. You know where we rode out yesterday, go show me how you'd tell we went through there."

She looked out at the lush meadow and blinked. She thought she remembered where they'd ridden off the gravel driveway... She started to walk along the hard packed road, looking at the slightly looser margin. Finally, she found a semi-circular mark. "Here, that's a horse track."

He nodded. "Keep going."

She walked into the grass, casting about for marks of their passage. A bruised stem of Indian paintbrush, knocked flat by a hoof, earned her a grin from Bes. She kept walking on, then stopped. He raised an eyebrow at her.

"Something else went through here." She pointed at the little marks the cut across the horses' trail.

"So it did. Go ahead and follow that, if you'd like."

Linn was curious, then in a few steps more down the slight slope in a wetter place, found the clear track she'd been seeking. "Oh, it was a deer!"

"Or an elk. Good sized herd nearby."

He straightened then, frowning. Linn felt it then... a deep strumming through her body. "What is that?" She cried out, looking toward the house. The kittens...

"Get to the house. The wards are breached." He spat out, already running for the barn. Linn took off for the house like a shot.

She came through the front door at a run, the kittens were still asleep on the couch. The house felt still and calm, in contrast to her racing heart. She caught her breath, then loaded the rifle that hung over the door. It might not help against a god, but it sure made her feel better. Looking out the window, she saw Bes saddling the horses.

He disappeared into the barn, then came back out with big saddle bags and lashed them on behind the saddles. Linn guessed they were for the kittens, but why not take the truck?

It occurred to her to wonder how her grandfather had traveled. She shook her head. The warning seemed to have settled into a low buzzing in her ears. Was it going to keep doing that, or did it mean more than one entity was passing through the barrier? Bes led the horses up to the porch and tied them there. He looked up and met her eyes and nodded. She took that to mean stay put.

She stood there at the window, the rifle in the crook of her arm and one hand on Lambent's pommel. One of the kittens was snoring behind her, making a little squeaky-toy noise. Suddenly she felt like crying. She didn't want them to be in danger, didn't want this to be happening.

She sucked in a deep breath and steadied herself. Nothing to be done about that now, just deal with it and soldier on, she told herself firmly. The waiting was the worst part.

Bes was out of sight when she saw the first thing emerge from the forest. She couldn't make out the shape or size of it, as it seemed to be covered in dark grey smoke. Then she realized she was Seeing it, the power coming off it was obscuring it on purpose. Bes came around the corner of the house, blazing white, and made a gesture at it, a ball of Power flying off his fingertips.

Then he turned and beckoned Linn out. She opened the door and stepped out. "Get the kittens." He ordered. She turned at once to scoop up Blackie. She couldn't really manage more than one at a time. He stretched and yawned.

She handed him to Bes and went back in the house, sparing a glance for the apparition that was still advancing. She thought there were three of them. She scooped up Spot One, and handed him off to Bes. It was as she turned to go back in the house a third time that she felt something hit her hard between the shoulder blades and knock her down. She was trying to get up when the house exploded.

Crying, Linn covered her head with her arms and waited until things had stopped landing on her before she looked up again. There was no fire, but the house was destroyed. The doorframe leaned crazily to the side and the wall was gone, in splinters. The kittens... She tried to crawl forward.

Bes scooped her up unceremoniously, throwing her over his shoulder. He carried her off the porch and shoved her onto her horse.

"Ride!" He bellowed at her, slapping the mare's rump hard. With a squeal, the horse bounded away from the house. Linn crouched over the neck of the running horse and held on for dear life. She didn't dare look back. She didn't know where she was going.

14

OLD BATTLES

Sekhmet was delighted to meet Steve at the end of the high path. They stropped cheeks in the cat equivalent to a human kiss, and walked slowly through Quetzalcoatl's gardens. They didn't talk for a while. Both knew the battle was coming, both were ready.

"Ever thought about what it must be like to be one of the Old Ones?" Steve finally asked.

Sekhmet looked at him. He sat back on his haunches and looked steadily back at her. She knew what he meant. "Yes, I've thought about it. And then I forgot, because that is our gift, you and I. To forget and stay young at heart and be able to laugh."

He flattened his ears in agreement. The Old Ones, the Olympians and the high Norse gods, had mostly forgotten to laugh, if they ever knew how. The weight of all the millennia they had seen, all the blood spilled, crushed them into solemnity. Maybe that was the reason behind this war. The absolute power they had wielded for so long left them unable to empathize with mortals.

She shook her head. "When we became gods, it was the beginning of our downfall."

He stood and started blindly down the paths again and she paced alongside him. "The blood spilled by us, and by our forefathers, can never be returned. I became so sickened by it, at the end... I retreated to the high plane entirely. Centuries passed before I returned to see what had become of my former home. Even today..." He looked at her and she could see a single crystal tear in his eye. As she watched it fell and hung trembling from a black whisker. "To the modern world, the blood spilled hangs over the people like a miasma and holds them back."

Sekhmet licked his cheek. He closed his eyes, and she washed his face until he started to purr. Then she pounced on him, nipping his ear as she vaulted over him. Instantly he was chasing her down the path, laughing. She let him catch her every so often, and they played like a pair of massive kittens until he had forgotten again.

Heff and Quetzalcoatl, watching from the palace, laughed.

"My garden may never be the same." The winged serpent said with a chuckle.

"It's worth it," the elder immortal replied. "The very human gift of laughter and play may save us yet."

"Yesss, the gift of curiosssity..." His hiss only showed up when he was stressed.

"The Old Ones never had it." Heff stated flatly. "I was born on this plane, yes, but I was partly raised in Olympus. They don't care. They don't like change, and they hate that humans are becoming a threat."

"So what are we doing?" rejoined the other, as if they hadn't been in council about this for weeks now.

"Fighting a delaying action. Waiting for a breakthrough that can stop the Old Ones. Looking for a way to kill an immortal."

Quetzalcoatl looked straight into Hephaestus' eyes. "You never said that in council."

"No." Heff replied bluntly. "You knew it, though."

The serpent nodded sinuously. "I guessed when you took the Scholar to sanctuary. And the Old Ones must suspect, as well, or they would not have sent minions to destroy her home. It was the opening salvo in this war."

Heff looked grim. "In the past we did not target our own kind. This time there will be no holds barred."

Quetzalcoatl tsk-ed at the other immortal. "You speak so much human slang."

Heff stiffened, looking off into the distance. He remained silent and the serpent saw him visibly pale.

"What is wrong?"

"The wards around my home have been breached."

"Go, then!"

There was a long hesitation, the god's shoulders tensed, his muscles rolling in a massive display of his strength, and then Heff's body slumped. "No, there is nothing I can do. It will take me too long to get there to be any good. I will send Sekhmet and Steve."

Quetzalcoatl lifted a wing and brushed his friend's arm with it. "I know it is hard. We need you here, though. You hold them together."

Heff's face looked as if it were cast in iron. "The general stays with his army. Even when his family is in danger. We need to gather all the children at the Sanctuary on Earth."

"All?" the serpent was startled.

"If they come after one, they will hunt them all. It is our weakest point."

The children of the gods, slow to mature into their Power, protected by gods and demi-gods all over the world, were the future. Raised as humans among humans they were intended to balance immortals and humans. Humans, after all, had sprung from immortals. Heff believed that with time, they would become intertwined and equal. He would live to see that, he had reason to believe, and he thought he would enjoy it.

The Old Ones liked their power, and would do anything to retain it. They might draw from the adulation of humans to feed their immense egos, but to them, humans were pawns in their ongoing battle for world domination. The children of the gods were none of theirs, these days, they had for centuries withdrawn to the citadel of Olympus.

Their withdrawal might be why humans had finally come into their birthright of joy and curiosity. Heff knew he and others who fostered human kind had also kick-started the renaissance of humanity. But it was the innate intelligence of the true children of the gods, humanity itself, sprung from the blood of the Titans, the first to slip through the cracks in the planes and come to Earth...

Heff tore himself from his wandering thoughts, closed his eyes and took a deep breath. He looked into the concerned rainbow-shot eyes of his friend and squared his shoulders. "I believe we have another planning committee to ride herd on."

He sent a sprite to summon Steve and Sekhmet to him. They met him at the entrance to the war chamber. He looked Sekhmet in the eyes and saw her fur lift along her entire spine.

"My wards were breached. Go quickly, and when you have determined the situation, all the children must be taken to Sanctuary below."

"All the children?"

"If they will attack ours, they will attack others who have not so doughty a protector."

Steve nodded grimly. "We run on the winds. Send sprites with us, that we may report back."

Heff sighed. "Thank you..."

Sekhmet licked his cheek and then they both turned and raced away, their long bodies almost touching the ground with each stride. Heff went into the room filled with a long conference table and immortals of every shape and description. It was utter chaos. All of them were talking at once and he shut the worry out of his mind and took control of the meeting.

15

FLIGHT

*L*inn could feel the rhythm of the galloping horse, but couldn't see where she was going any more, she was crying too hard. She wiped at her face angrily with her sleeve. It wouldn't help Blackie and Spot One for them to fall into a ravine or something. She did wish that she knew where they were headed, though. She was hoping Bes had guided the horse with his power, or something.

They had ridden out of the valley and the mare slowed and turned to climb up the low ridge that separated this valley from the next. Linn let her take the lead. She could sit up in the saddle now and take stock. She ached all over. Blackie and Spot One were both curled in the panniers, sound asleep. That had to be Bes' doing.

But the house had been blown apart, by whatever those things had been. With two of her kittens inside. The tears started to flow again and she rubbed them away. Bes was still back there, outnumbered. She couldn't go back... the kittens were her first priority. It had only been maybe a half hour since he'd sent her to safety, but running the horse any further would have been insanity.

She rubbed the mare's sweaty neck. The golden horse flipped an ear back at her, then focused on the trail ahead. Linn looked around. There was a trail, a faint one, through the sparse trees of the high forest they were making their way through. She didn't know where they were going, but the mare did. Linn was going to trust that, for now.

She looked up at the sky. The sun was still high. They could travel for another couple of hours, then she would need to set up camp. Which meant by then they needed to get down the other side of this ridge and find water. She wasn't going to urge the horse to go any faster, though. Only in movies and on TV did you make your horses run for hours. In real life, that would leave you on foot, with a dead horse.

She took stock of what they had. One fourteen-year-old girl, who knew probably just enough bushcraft to get them all in trouble, one enchanted horse (she hoped), two comatose kittens, blanket roll on the back of the saddle, her belt kit, and Lambent, a magical sword. Her survival pack was back in the barn. There hadn't been time to get it.

The sky was clear and it didn't rain here often in the summer. That was a plus. Downside, it was going to get cool tonight. The mare was climbing higher into the mountains, and Linn started to look for signs of water. There was a waterskin strapped to the saddle, under her leg, she discovered. Bes had saddled with the intention of them riding quite a while, she guessed.

No milk for the kittens, no food for her beyond the protein bar in her belt kit. No rifle. Lambent was a sword. Useless out here, except for chopping kindling. She was going to have to figure out how to catch some rabbits. She was twisting around in the saddle looking at everything when the mare shifted tacks.

Linn grabbed at the saddle horn and looked ahead. They were headed down into a narrow valley now, and.... she squinted. That looked like a stream ahead. She was going to drink out of it, giardia or no. She'd read there were some high mountain streams that weren't infected with it. Not that she had a choice, the water treatment system was in her survival kit.

The mare picked up speed as they neared the little rocky stream, and then stopped at the verge of it to lower her head and drink deeply. Linn slowly slipped out of the saddle, gasping as she hit the ground. She was sore in places she didn't think she'd had before today.

Linn stood by the drinking horse for a moment, letting the blood return to her legs. She rubbed her butt. It was numb at the moment. She lifted the waterskin off the saddle and knelt to fill it at the clear stream. Behind her, Blackie poked his head up out of the saddlebag and looked around, his ears flattened to his head. He wasn't happy.

Linn heard his miaow and went to him. She took him water in her cupped hands, which he lapped gratefully. He didn't seem willing to leave the cozy saddle bag, so she went round to the other and patted Spot One until he woke up, too. He lifted his head up and look around, then stretched out a paw to bat at her loosened hair. Linn kissed his nose and went to get him water as well.

The kittens cared for, she stood for a moment to take stock of her surroundings. She was lost, she knew that. She'd been in too much of a panic to take a compass sighting when they left, so she pulled it out now and looked around. No real visible landmarks. The stream ran to the West, a little to the south. If she followed it down, she would probably reach civilization.

Linn thought about that for a moment. Even if she did get to a town, with people, what would happen? Her grandfather was missing, who knows what had happened to Bes. Her mother was trying to keep the world from blowing up. Her grandmother was too far away. Linn pulled out her phone. No service, which she'd thought. She turned it off to save the battery and slipped it back into her shirt pocket, buttoning it carefully. She might need it.

For now, she would stay with the mare's trail. She did seem to be going somewhere, and Linn knew horses tended to go home, left to themselves. Perhaps then, the mare would take them to Coyote. She wasn't sure she wanted to meet him. The legends she'd read were wild. But he would know how to get her to her grandfather, and he was Bes' friend.

She looked at the mare, who was ready to go again, and decide she'd walk for a while. Holding the reins, she let the horse have her head, and they set off again, following the stream. Linn limped a little until her muscles loosened up, and when they came to a shallow place where the mare wanted to ford, she remounted. She wanted to stay near water, but it wasn't time to stop, yet. She didn't know how far it was to Coyote's, but Bes had gotten there and back in an afternoon with the truck.

Back in the saddle, Linn relaxed a little and felt how tired she was. Her bones ached. Her everything hurt. The horse was headed uphill again... On a winding, easy way, but discernibly up to the top of the ridge. What lay behind that was anybody's guess. Blackie pulled himself out of the saddlebag and, much to her dismay, made his way delicately into her lap. There he sat tall, looking in every direction.

"This is a high forest." Linn told him, her voice hoarse from crying and not having spoken for a while. "The trees are spaced pretty far apart because it's cold, and there's not a lot of rainfall."

The kitten flicked an ear back in her direction. Linn knew he was listening, but wasn't sure how much he understood.

"I love the smell." she told him, sniffing deeply. The forest smelled spicy, pungent with the resin of the spruce and fir trees they rode under. The kitten opened his mouth and she knew he was using the Jacobsen's organ that allowed cats to smell very acutely, almost tasting the air.

Linn ruffled his ears. "No fair. I can't smell as much as you."

Blackie leaned against her chest and purred briefly, slitting his eyes. She sighed. She was the one who should be comforting him, and instead he was helping her. She'd lost his siblings... She wiped her eyes and promised herself that she would always carry a handkerchief from now on. Her sleeve was disgusting.

"It's starting to get late. As soon as we get to the bottom of the next valley we'll stop for the night. I'm afraid there won't be any milk."

Blackie was back to sitting upright, Linn could see his claws sinking into the leather of the saddle, as the mare scrambled up a slope to the ridgeline. She put her arms around him and held onto the saddlehorn and the kitten. He headbutted her jawline affectionately.

Linn turned in the saddle to look at Spot One, who was watching the world go by alertly from his bag. He mewed at her, a raspy sound. She looked down into the valley.

"One more slope, and then we stop. It's not going to be comfortable, but I'll keep you safe." Linn wished she felt as confident as she sounded. She was exhausted, and had no illusions about being able to use Lambent against an attacker, much less three of them. But she'd try. She squared her shoulders and sent the mare down the slope, letting the tired beast pick her way slowly.

The bottom of the valley held a tiny intermittent stream that held a few puddles of water, enough for the mare to get another good drink. Linn decided that she'd boil the water if she used any here. She unsaddled the horse, who immediately found a dry, flat area and rolled luxuriously in the pine needle carpet. The kittens sat near the saddle, watching the big creature flop around warily.

Linn unrolled the bundle that had been tied behind the saddle. An eight-foot oilskin tarp, a ground cloth, and a down sleeping bag were revealed, along with enough rope to set up a small shelter. Linn drew Lambent and went looking for a good spot. She used the leaf-bladed sword to cut a slender sapling for a ridgepole, wincing as the merry dancing flickers of power bit deeply into wood. It seemed wrong, somehow, to use her sword for this.

She chose two trees that were about ten feet apart and lashed the pole she'd cut to them at about head height to herself. Then she attached the tarp to it, angling it back to the ground. What little wind was coming down the valley would be deflected off them by the tarp. She chosen a slight slope toward the creek, close enough to the creek to build her fire in the rocky verge of the dry creek bed, where she was sure she wouldn't start a forest fire. As she started the little blaze, she could almost hear her grandfather's voice in her head telling her: "you planning on roasting an ox, or just staying warm?"

Linn sighed. They'd be warm, if hungry. Her tummy growled. She spread out her ground cloth and bag, and brought the kittens from the saddle, where they had stayed. They seemed to think it was a part of home. She could see their uncertainty in how they moved, and how they stayed close to each other, or her when she was still enough.

She broke a chunk of her protein bar off and offered a piece to each of them. They both sniffed and then gave her identical looks of disgust. Linn chuckled a little. "Sorry, boys, it's what I've got tonight."

Blackie turned and started to wash his brother.

"I guess that's a no." Linn ate the protein bar. "How about some water?"

That they deigned to lap from her cupped hands. She gave them the water from the waterskin. She would have to find some birch bark so she could boil water before she'd use it from the puddles. And that would have to wait until morning. She didn't want to go wandering around in the dark.

Pushing a stick a little further into the fire and watching the sparks dance, Linn pulled her boots off and crawled into the sleeping bag. The kittens crept in on either side of her. She lay on her side looking at the fire, and slipped into sleep.

She didn't dream at all that night. She awakened to a cold nose on her cheek, followed by a raspy tongue washing her face. Spluttering, she opened her eyes. Blackie was draped over her chest bathing her. Spot One was a warm lump curled at the small of her back. Blackie started to purr.

"Poor baby." Linn cuddled him in her arms. "You must be hungry, and wondering where your sisters are."

She looked over to the fire, surprised to see that it was still alight. Then she saw the two rabbits hanging from her ridgepole. She sat up into the cold air, clutching Blackie, and looked around. The forest was empty and quiet in the dawn light. There were birds singing, and a far off chatter of a squirrel, but no movement.

Shivering a little, Linn climbed out of the sleeping bag and went to look at the carcasses. They had been killed with an arrow, she thought, shot through the heart, and then gutted and skinned. Tied with a bit of rawhide and hung over the ridgepole for her and the kittens' breakfast. She looked around. No sign anywhere, and nothing moving, as before. Still, she raised her voice and called "Thank you!"

Leaving the kittens curled up in the warm sleeping bag, she cut a couple of sticks to cook the rabbits over the fire. Whoever had left her the rabbits had also pushed her sticks in and kept the fire going. As she prepared them, she stretched and tried to work the kinks out of her muscles. She might be young, but yesterday had been a very long day indeed.

The mare wandered over to have her nose patted. Linn loved the velvety feel of it and hugged the palomino's neck for a minute, picking twigs and pine needles out of her mane. She didn't have a curry comb, but she grabbed a handful of the long green pine needles and wadded them up and tried that. She didn't know how much good it did, but the mare sighed and leaned into her, so it was making her happy, at least.

She stopped when she could smell the rabbit, and rinsed her hands in a puddle. The pine pitch was there to stay, but the horse hair she could get rid of. Poking the rabbit with her knife, she decided it was done enough. The kittens had ventured close enough to the fire to worry her about their whiskers. She cut the rabbit in half and offered them the parts. Blackie took it eagerly and carried it off to the side before beginning to chew on it. Spot One sniffed, licked, and then seized it. She watched both of them, worried they'd choke on a bone.

She ate hers much more delicately, as hungry as she was. The kittens were done before she was, and she cut a few bits of hers for them. While they were nosing about exploring, she broke down camp and made sure the fire was extinguished.

She thought she knew who had looked after them in the night, and wondered why he didn't show himself. The mare stood docilely while she hefted the saddle on with difficulty. She hadn't done much of the saddling before, and hadn't been paying close enough attention the night before. Fortunately, the mare was content to just stand there and let her fiddle with the girth until she'd figured it out.

Tying the blanket roll and panniers on took a little more time. She was very warm by the time she turned to the kittens, who were pouncing on one another and wrestling. Linn sighed. Bes' trick with the sleeping would come in handy about now. She tried to pick up Blackie, who danced away from her, obviously thinking she was joining the game.

Spot One pounced on her foot, attacking her boot laces, and she captured him.

He wriggled, wanting down.

"Sorry, little guy. We can't stay here. Time to travel on."

She put him in the saddle bag and he gave her a reproachful look, but stayed put. Blackie climbed her leg, making her yelp as his claws caught her.

"Be nice!" she told him as she took him around to the other bag. "Stay there, now."

Getting on the horse without kicking the kitten in the face was interesting. She muttered under her breath as she settled. Checking her lashings one last time, she kicked the mare gently. The palomino looked around at Linn, and then pricked her ears forward, looking up the valley. Linn gave the mare her head and they began moving slowly uphill again. Linn wondered how high into the Bitterroots they were going to go.

It was another lovely summer day. Idaho in the summer rarely gets too warm, and in the cover of the trees it was comfortable. Linn drowsed in the saddle, trusting her horse to know the way. The kittens had gone to sleep with full bellies.

Around noon she dismounted and walked alongside the horse for an hour. The mare showed no signs of slowing, but Linn didn't want to hurt her, either. She held onto the stirrups during a steep scramble up a slope, but mostly just tried to keep up. She stopped seeing much of the scenery, as her world narrowed to the next copse of trees, the next slope. They were traveling mostly east, but also slightly north, so they were crossing ridges and valleys.

Sometime in the afternoon she decided they weren't headed to Coyote's place. It wouldn't have taken Bes that little time to pick up the horses if his lair were this remote. She was tired, the mare was tired. Linn patted her neck. "Good girl. Thank you for the ride."

The mare just flicked an ear back at the crazy human. Linn wondered how much further they could all go on like this. It was early, but she thought maybe they would camp at the next water. If the horse became incapacitated, she and the kittens would be in dire straits.

She dismounted as they reached the crest of the ridge and climbed up ahead of the mare, worried the horse would fall on her or kick her. At the top she stopped and panted a minute while the mare joined her in a last scrabble of hooves on rocks. Then she looked down into the valley she realized she had been right the first time. They had found Coyote.

16

COYOTE'S HOME

*L*inn remounted the mare and realized she'd lost the tired feeling as they rode slowly down the slope, the horse picking her way through the enormous bones that littered the entire valley. She knew where they were headed, now. The long alligator shaped skull at the head of the valley with a curl of smoke issuing from one nostril had to be Coyote's home. She knew the story, how Coyote had rescued the Niimipuu, who would later be called the Nez Perce, from a gigantic monster, she just hadn't realized it was literal.

She wondered if magic masked this valley from mortal eyes. Surely it would have been in the news, this valley of bones, if a satellite could see into it. Blackie crept into her lap again, as he had done the day before. Linn wrapped an arm around him, grateful for his solid warmth.

There was little green growing in the valley, as though it had been blighted and never recovered. The bones loomed overhead as they reached the floor of the valley and the ribcage. Linn studied them. White, cracked, and incredibly ancient looking. She shivered a little. The monster who had died here had been bigger than any dinosaur, even.

They reached the skull, and she saw that a rickety staircase led to one nostril, and the smoke vented from the other. No-one came to greet them, but the mare stepped livelier as they drew near, tossing her head a little.

Linn saw something off to one side that somehow made her relax a little. A small, neatly tended garden in square raised beds flourished, with flowers mixed in with vegetables.

The horse went right through the gap between teeth. The canine of the monster loomed next to Linn's shoulder like a massive ivory column, and then they were in the gloom. The horse stopped. Linn's eyes adjusted to the dim light and she saw stalls built against the wall of the upper jaw. The lower jaw was gone altogether, she realized.

She slid off the mare, feeling her legs wobble. Then the buckskin gelding put his head over his stall door and whickered to the mare. The mare moved to bump noses with him and Linn, taken off guard, lost her balance and sat down abruptly. If the buckskin was here, then Bes must be as well.

Blackie leaped out of the saddle bag and ran to where Linn was still sitting on the earth floor of the stable. He bumped her chest with his head, and she hugged him.

"I'm ok. Just tired." She told him. He touched his nose to hers, and then Spot One joined him and did so as well. Linn slowly got to her feet and went to the mare. She loosened the saddle and slid it off, setting it on a nearby rack. Everything was rustic but clean. She opened the stall next to the mare's and the horse walked in and pulled a mouthful of hay out of the manger. Linn closed the door and walked back outside, the kittens following on her heels.

The breeze tugged at her hair as she stood by the gigantic tooth, looking out into the eerie valley. She' had braided it that morning, but it hadn't been brushed. She felt grubby and tired. She let out a deep breath and focused. The landscape in front of her lit with Power. The grass-green flickers of the Coyote mingled with deep umber that was weird.

Linn blinked and closed her eyes. She thought what she had just Seen was the Monster's power. It had to be, even though it had been dead for something like three millennia. She shivered in the warm air, her neck hair raising.

Blackie put his paws on her knee and she looked down into his baby blue eyes. She wondered what color they would be when he was grown up. She started to focus on him, to See if his power was coming in, and then stopped. She was just too tired.

Spot One walked over to the stairs, tail held high, and started up them. Linn followed to keep him safe and out of mischief, if nothing else. Together the little group went up the side of the skull and along a long deck to the opening of the nostril, which had been closed in and had a door in the center.

A scrawled note was tacked to the door. She pulled it off and squinted at it. "Come in and be comfortable." It read. The handwriting was terrible. She turned the knob and went inside.

17

HIGH PATH TO THE LOW

Sekhmet stayed on the high path longer than she would have ordinarily. The closer they drew to the earth's surface the more power it took to run the path. Finally, she let it go, and they fell to earth, buoyed by the Power. Steve remained at her side, unspeaking. She appreciated his respect for her fear.

She ran through the wards without stopping, feeling the tickle of recognition as they were already attuned to her. Steve, beside her, yelped but didn't break stride. She looked over at him, and he just shook his head. The Ward's warning sting didn't do damage, it was just uncomfortable. Heff attuned them to very few, suspicious old man.

They ran on, down the driveway, two great cats in perfect step. Sekhmet faltered as she saw what was left of Heff's house. Only the side walls still stood, the front and rear walls were completely gone. Debris scattered all over the meadow behind the house. Nothing moved in the devastation.

Sekhmet roared, hearing Steve's eerie shriek sound at the same time. She leapt up onto what was left of the porch and sniffed. Steve prowled through the flowerbeds with his nose to the ground. He called up to her.

"Bes was here, and three of Mars' golems."

A movement from the barn caught her eye, and she saw Bes stagger out into the sunlight. He was holding something. Sekhmet leaped toward him, transforming to human in mid leap and landing on pointed foot. Some things could not be done with four paws. She caught him as he stumbled and then Steve was beside her, helping. They eased Bes onto the bench by the pump.

"Sorry, Hathor." The diminutive god said, looking up at Sekhmet and using her other name. "They imprinted on Linn."

He unwrapped the afghan and revealed two toddlers, asleep and hugging one another. One had black curly hair, and the other pretty strawberry blonde ringlets. They looked to be about three years old.

"Oh, Bes..." Sekhmet gathered them into her arms, waking them in the transfer. They blinked at her. The redhead put her thumb in her mouth.

Steve hugged Bes. "How can we thank you? and are you all right?" The emotional Latino had the other's head between his palms, looking closely at him.

"Leggo of me, you lothario." Bes grumbled. "Just a bit tired."

"They were dead and you brought them back."

"I knew she'd kill me if I didn't." Bes tried to joke. "and they weren't dead. Just disassociated for a time." He wasn't clear if he meant Linn or Sekhmet by the 'she' and it didn't matter.

Sekhmet, cuddling the girls and kissing each of them, looked at him over their heads. "Thank you. For them to have been in that state for too long would have destroyed their minds."

Steve took the girls, who wouldn't let the adults separate them. They looked up at him for a minute solemnly, and then cuddled on his chest. He smiled down at them. Sekhmet turned to Bes. "We cannot stay. Hephaestus tasked us with protecting all the children."

Bes blinked at her, his fatigue showing on his face and in his reactions. "I sent Linn and the other two babies to Coyote."

Sekhmet rubbed her face. "Oh, my. You do know he's bughouse crazy?"

"He's also my friend." Bes offered softly and without offense at her blunt words. "He will make sure they are safe. He may be the most powerful immortal in North America at this time."

Steve interjected. "We need you to go to the Sanctuary and set it up. We'll be sending the children to you."

Bes nodded. "I will get Linn and these four there and be ready. How many?"

Sekhmet shook her head. "I don't know. Not more than a dozen, I think."

"That few." He shook his head. "The Old Ones have a blind spot. They can't rule the world unless they multiply. And they stopped doing that a long time ago."

Sekhmet knew Bes wasn't one of the Old Ones. He was, if possible, even older than they. But he thought differently than they did. He'd protected humans for as long as she had known him. She stood and transformed back to cat. She put her face up to his. He lifted an eyebrow at her. She breathed on him, sending a wave of Power with her warm air. Bes put a hand on either side of her face.

"Go with the wind, Hathor." His blessing, invoking the gentler side of the two-faced goddess, made her smile. In cat form, that had an interesting effect of baring her fangs.

"I will not release Sekhmet until needed." She promised, acknowledging that her other name left carnage in her wake.

He released her, and Steve stepped closer to Bes and handed the toddlers over. "I trust you will take care of them." He spoke solemnly.

The Jaguar god transformed, and like his mate, breathed into Bes' face. Bes closed his eyes. "You need a mint, man."

Steve laughed. "See you soon." He growled in response.

The pair loped down the drive. Bes, feeling the power they had given him renewing his strength, looked down at the toddlers. "I need to get car seats, don't I?"

He looked after the now distant cats. "I need to be ready, too." He knew what they would bring him would be a passel of very challenging creatures. The children of gods were never easy.

One of the toddlers grabbed his beard and giggled. He kissed the top of her head. "You two are easy. Linn is easy. Some of these kids are going to be a handful."

She burbled at him while her quieter sister just smiled. Neither of them had said a word yet. They were only two days old, though, in human form. They wouldn't let the other out of their sight, and could walk a little. He needed Linn's help.

"Let's go, then."

He walked toward the truck, carrying them in the afghan. He didn't look back at the destruction of Heff's home. Time enough to deal with it when the war was won. He'd let the goats free, and the chickens, to fend for themselves. With the wards still in place, they should be safe enough.

He pulled a phone out of his pocket and dialed.

"Hey, old friend. I'm on my way."

"You are much anticipated, Bes." Her voice sounded in his ear.

"I have to collect Linn and the kittens, then we will get on a plane to you."

"We will be ready. A charter flight will meet you once you are in Boise."

"Thank you."

"No, Bes... thank you. You have been the protector of us all. The future lies in your hands."

He pulled out of the driveway. "Sometimes I wonder about that, Pele. All I can do is make sure the children are safe."

"It is enough."

He shut the phone off and looked at the sleeping children. He'd tucked them into the passenger foot space and had them sleep for now. Even if they were in an accident they were protected by his Power. And immortal. His mouth quirked up a little. He needed a minivan and car seats. This is why he side-lined as a god of war and vengeance, to keep his man card current.

At least in the modern age he didn't wear kilts any more. In Egypt they were great in the heat. Here in Idaho, he'd freeze. Sekhmet, earlier, in human form, had taken on the dress he remembered her best in, the flowing white cotton gowns of early Egypt. She'd been really upset about the children, he thought. She normally wore whatever was current fashion. Which was probably why the attackers had come here, trying to undermine the leaders of the opposition.

When he turned off the main road, onto a meandering dirt track that looked like a logging access road partly because it was one, he focused his wandering thoughts on what he was doing. This was a tricky drive. Usually, Coyote met him halfway. Bes wasn't entirely sure it was drivable the whole way, although the mad god had said it was.

He hit a pothole and bounced almost to the roof of the truck. A glance at the sleeping children showed them cushioned by his bubble of power. He grunted and paid attention to the trail again. He hoped the four-wheel drive would handle it all the way to the end, he didn't fancy walking in with two toddlers in tow.

He slowed to a crawl as the track wound up the ridgeline. Linn had been gone for three days now. He knew she should have reached Coyote's valley yesterday, but he hadn't heard anything from her through him.

"Where are you, Trickster?" Bes muttered, trying to avoid the worst of the potholes and emerging saplings in the road.

The trail led down into the next valley. Bes had never come to it this way, and he wondered if Coyote had wards. He'd only been here a few times, always with Heff, or Coyote. He knew the Coyote was strong, but not if he was strong enough to dispense with protections. The trail was steep, and he felt uncomfortably like the truck was about to slip and go tobogganing down the hillside.

At the bottom of the valley, he stopped for a minute and mopped his forehead. He was sweating. He slipped the truck back in gear and started forward, cautiously. The truck started to roll forward, then he hit the brakes and stared at the massive wall of umber scales that had materialized in front of them.

They shifted and slid, and he realized he was looking at the tail of a dragon. He looked up, and the head of the monster loomed into view.

"Greetings, Bes." the bass vibrato seemed to shake the bones of the earth beneath his feet.

"Hot damn, I thought all of you were dead." Bes blurted out before he could stop it. Dragons were notoriously short on their senses of humor.

The dragon laughed until he shook the ground. Bes fell to one knee, catching himself on one hand before more of him hit the dirt. That had to have registered on the Richter scale. He looked up at the glowing breath of the massive mouth that had come closer yet. A surprisingly delicate, snake like tongue flickered out at him.

"I must disappoint you, I'm afraid. I am quite dead."

Bes stood up and dusted off his hands. "It feels like you're here."

"My power lingers on."

Bes' vision flickered, and he could see a blasted valley littered with whitened bones, then the great Dragon was solid again. No wonder the Coyote lived here. No immortal could enter this place without permission.

"My charge came here?"

"Ah, yes, the intrepid ones. They are with me since yesterday. Safe, and even comfortable."

Bes laughed. "She is intrepid." he agreed, then let out a heartfelt sigh. "I'm glad they made it safely. I need to take them with me, though."

"Do you, now?" The dragon rested his chin on his tail, regarding the short god. "Why do you need to take them out into this dangerous world you have created?"

"I created?"

"Oh, you know what I mean." the dragon chuckled and Bes felt a wash of warm, sulfur-scented air brush over him. His hair stood on end all over his body. It had been countless millennia since he'd felt a dragon's breath. The enormous monster went on. "You were one of the first to come to this world. One of those who changed what it might have been, into what it is now."

"I was among those first arrivals. I fought the changes, and have stood protector all the time since then. And you... you are not of this world, either." Bes challenged, fearlessly.

"I was not. But now I have lain here for so long that I am more of this earth than you are. My power is seeped into the the rocks and soil here, and it is all under my protection. What more can you offer the little ones?"

"I will take them to Linnaea's grandmother. We gather all the children in a sanctuary for their protection and I will need Linn to help me."

The dragon contemplated him with glowing amber eyes for a very long time. Bes waited patiently. It had been a very long time since he'd talked to a dragon, but he remembered not to rush them.

"All the children." the great apparition sighed finally. "When have we had to protect the children from ourselves? They are such a precious and rare gift."

"Yes, they are."

"In the place we came from, such a thing would be unthinkable."

"We have been so long gone from there, and warped by power and time. I wonder if any of us are still sane."

The dragon laughed again, throwing his head back. "I am certain I am not, now. Or if I was ever. Dreaming, I have eaten the people. Dreaming, I woke to a new reality. I dreamt I was back home, soaring the yellow skies of our home..." He dropped his head until his nose was almost touching Bes. His voice broke through the stocky immortal, who rode the rolling earth like the deck of a ship. "I woke to find myself imprisoned here, under blue skies, surrounded by the green hills of Earth. No, small one, I am not sane."

"Do you want to go home again?"

The dragon pulled back, rearing up until his head was over the surrounding mountains. Bes was glad he was the only one that could see this. Then he folded back down on himself and slid away, the massive tail leaving no marks as it moved away from the road. Like the wind through the trees, Bes heard the dragon's response.

"Yessss..."

18

SANCTUARY

*L*inn stepped through the door into the skull of the monster, looking around. The dome of the skull vaulted overhead, creamy ivory in color. The floor was wide boards, smooth and painted ochre. Scattered about the big, open room were a woodstove, kitchen table and chairs, bookshelves, and a huge canopy bed. She walked over to the stove, feeling the warmth and smelling the stew on it.

Her stomach growled. Blackie did the meerkat thing, sitting up on his haunches and sniffing hard. He was adorable, and she felt the same way about the rich, savory smell. Linn looked around for cupboards and bowls. The kittens were served first, and practically dove into their bowls. Linn opted for a spoon and a seat at the big table.

Looking around, she saw details she hadn't noticed at first. There was a door at the back of the room. She was hoping for an indoor bathroom and possibly even a shower. The house was divided into rough quadrants, she realized. The kitchen, a sitting area, the bedroom, and a library...

Leaving her empty bowl on the table for the moment, she walked over to the shelves that lined one wall. Much like her grandfather's library, but more extensive. History, both European and Asian in addition to the expected volumes on Native American history. Fiction... Coyote was a big science fiction fan. Linn pulled a dog-eared copy of one of her favorites,

"The Moon is a Harsh Mistress" off the shelf. Opening it, she found it was signed by Robert Heinlein. Reverently, she was sliding it back on the shelf when a voice behind her made her jump.

"'Funny once', I still have trouble with that concept."

Linn turned quickly, to see a sandy-yellow coyote sitting by the table and laughing, his long pink tongue lolling out. Blackie pounced on his tail and she gasped. The god just laughed harder and rolled over to play with the kittens. Spot One grabbed the nearest ear, and Coyote wrestled with him, growling softly. One Linn could tell they were playing, she relaxed.

Avoiding the furball of bodies on the floor, she gathered bowls and took them to the sink, which had an ordinary faucet. Tentatively, she turned the mixer lever. Water flowed out. Coyote looked up from the floor, where he had Blackie pinned with a paw to the head.

"I'm not as old-school as your grandfather is, chickie." Blackie twisted away from him and ran, Coyote on his tail. Spot One pounced from the seat of a chair where he had been lurking and tripped the immortal.

Linn laughed and washed the dishes. They were still mock-fighting when she was done, and as she watched them, she realized what Coyote was doing. Teaching the kittens how to fight. She'd been thinking of them as babies, but they were growing so fast. She wondered if all immortal children matured this quickly.

She put a hand on Lambent's pommel. She had been learning, too. How to run, mostly. And how to survive.

"Where is Bes?" She asked Coyote. He answered without looking up from the edge of the couch. Spot One had flattened himself and scooted under it.

"On his way. The gelding came home by himself just a few hours before you got here. Of course, he was able to travel faster without a burden."

"How do you know, then?" She asked curiously.

"I know everything that happens on my land." He sounded utterly sure, and suddenly she wondered how far the extent of his land stretched.

Linn sat down, arranging Lambent to hang properly. He knew everything... "Then why did you let us be attacked? The other two kittens were killed!"

"Knowing and being able to act on are two different things. I was able to keep an eye on you as you came here, once I intersected you." He padded over, leaving the two kittens wrestling with one another. Putting his front paws on Linn's knees, he reached up and kissed her face with his long wet tongue. Linn's giggle was watery with her tears.

"I am sorry for your grief, child." He spoke softly, his golden eyes fixed on hers.

She hugged his neck, feeling the soft ruff of fur. "I was supposed to be their guardian!" she wailed. She felt him shift abruptly and opened her eyes. He'd changed to human form, and was holding her gently, kneeling on the floor. Long black braids fell over his shoulders, and a peaceful face that looked as though it were made of old leather looked at her. He was wearing a buckskin shirt and jeans. His feet were bare.

"Cry it out. You will feel better."

Linn sniffled. "I'm ok."

He nodded. "You saved two of them. Bes is not dead. You are not dead. It is a victory."

"No, it's not..." Linn felt the tears coming back. "I left them behind."

"I, too, have left many behind." Coyote hugged her. Linn cried on his shoulder. She remembered the last time she had cried like this. After her father's death, she had crawled into her mother's lap, and they had both cried until they fell asleep. Linn couldn't bear losing the little ones. Not again. She couldn't do anything about it, though.

Coyote picked her up and carried her to the couch. He tucked her in with one of her grandmother's afghans, she recognized the pattern. She clutched at it and whispered, "thank you."

He kissed her forehead and said, "Sleep, sweet child. You have ventured much and will win more than you know."

Linn felt as though she were falling into a well. She clutched at his sleeves, and then everything slipped away. First Bes, now Coyote. Drat them. She was going to have to learn how to counter the sleep spell. As soon as she woke up...

When she woke up she realized the sun was shining. She looked up and saw what she hadn't the evening before. Where the eyes of the monster had been were two great windows. She looked back down to see

Spot One lying across her legs. She twisted her head around and realized that Blackie was draped over the arm of the couch, one paw on her head. She felt warm and safe. She closed her eyes and drifted off again.

She woke up to the smell of bacon and eggs. She sat up and rubbed her eyes. Coyote was standing at the stove, stirring something in a skillet. The kittens were at his feet eating already, tails straight up in the air. The immortal looked over his shoulder at her.

"Shower while you can and then come and get it... You have a long day ahead."

Linn stretched and staggered toward the bathroom. She had been in it briefly the night before. Now, she found that he had a towel and clothes laid out waiting for her. Gratefully, she got clean and dressed. They were too big for her, but they were clean.

Coyote nodded when she came out. "Good, you were getting pretty ripe, kid." He teased.

He put a plate down and Linn sat gladly to eat. He had cooked the bacon, then chopped it and added it and some tomatoes and herbs to the scrambled eggs. It tasted like heaven. She giggled a little. Coyote sat down and looked at her quizzically.

"Food of the gods." She explained. "Ambrosia. I never thought it would look like this."

He laughed. "It is good to feed a hungry child again. I had forgotten how satisfying it was to cook for someone who appreciates your food."

"Well, I like it. You can feed me anytime." She finished the last bite and took the plate to the sink.

"What are we doing today?" she asked Coyote.

"You are going to take it easy and perhaps read. My library is yours." He instructed her.

"And you?" she asked curiously.

"I prepare to join your grandfather." His voice was solemn.

"You will leave your land?"

"I must, this time. I never go, but this time I am needed."

"It's bad... isn't it." Linn heard her voice tremble. She gulped. She wasn't a little girl, and she wasn't going to cry again.

"It could be. But we will stop them. Your grandfather is formidable."

"This has happened before." She knew that from some things her grandfather had hinted at.

His eyes focused on something very far away indeed. "On a small scale, so many times. On a grander scale, the world has been rolled back to the stone age a handful of times. That... that is what they want this time."

"What can we do?" Linn felt very small and young again. She had been feeling very confident after her trek.

"You and Bes are going to keep the children safe."

"I hate babysitting." She hadn't been all that good at it, so far.

Coyote laughed. He did that a lot, she had noticed. "The children of the immortals are the key to the future of the earth. You have proved your worth..."

Linn felt her lip wobble. She bit it and listened hard, trying not to think about what she had left behind.

"You are a child yourself, but this is an important task."

Linn nodded, not trusting her voice.

Coyote stood. "I'll be in the stable if you need me."

Linn sat looking up and out of the eye of the monster for a long time. The kittens were asleep on the couch. Finally, she stood and went to find a book. Today she wanted something to make her laugh. Coyote could, and she could learn. She had a feeling it was an important survival skill.

She was curled up with a kitten on her feet and the afghan wrapped around her when Bes walked in the door. She shrieked and ran to him, hugging him hard. He staggered back a little, laughing.

"Oof! Girl, I'm immortal, not unbreakable." He hugged her back hard, though.

"I thought I'd never see you again!" She sniffed as she realized she was crying.

"I have a surprise for you." He put her a little away from him.

"What?" Linn was trying not to cry.

"Close your eyes."

Obediently, Linn closed her eyes. She heard the door open again, and then a soft, warm, wiggly bundle was in her arms. Her eyes flew open and she cried out.

"Kittens!" she stopped abruptly. Coyote gave her the other toddler.

Linn looked down at the little girls in confusion. "Who are they?"

"Patches and Spot Two."

Linn protested, shaking her head. "They're human!"

The redhead put her arms around Linn's neck and cuddled. Spot Two cooed up at her.

"They don't talk quite yet."

"They are *human*." She repeated.

Coyote sighed. "They are immortals. When they were killed in the house..."

"What!?" Linn looked at him, horrified.

"They died in the blast. Their bodies were destroyed. Their consciousness was not. They are the children of two immortals and possess the power to revive in a formed body."

"But their imprinting dictated the form. And they think of you as mother, right now." Bes finished.

Linn looked down at the sweet faces. Her mind was reeling. "They are alive." she whispered, finally.

She took them over to the couch and sat down. Blackie sat up and yawned, showing his fangs. Then he sniffed Patches and mewed at her. She hugged his neck. Linn looked up at Bes and Coyote, aware that tears were silently falling down her cheeks.

"I can't keep calling them Patches and Spot." she said. Coyote shook his head and chuckled.

"You think of names. Plan to stay here tonight, we'll leave in the morning." Bes patted Spot One, who was trying to climb the short god. He'd gotten too big to do it, though.

Linn nodded and buried her face in Spot Two's hug. The child was wearing a simple dress and no shoes. Her tumbled ringlets badly needed a brushing. She didn't look at all like the kitten Linn knew, but she felt right.

Linn looked at her. "You all need names that mean something."

Blackie headbutted her cheek. "I know you like your name." Linn assured him.

She looked at the black-haired child. "Moira. You are Moira."

The little girl smiled at her and then grabbed Blackie. Linn let her wiggle out of her arms and down to the floor. She picked up Patches and hoisted the redhead up in the air. The little girl squealed and kicked.

"Patricia. Close to what it was before."

Linn put her down and turned to Spot One, who was sitting next to her with his tail wrapped around his feet.

"And you?"

He opened his mouth in a soundless meow. She stroked his head and he arched his jaw into her palm.

"I just named one sister for the Fates, and the other for a Roman high society. What shall we do for you? Your mother is Sekhmet, also called Hathor. Your father has an unpronounceable name and prefers to be called Steve."

He just looked at her, purring.

"You're no help. I need a baby name book."

She got up and walked over to the bookcase. No baby name books - she would have been shocked - but there was another copy of the Standard Dictionary of Folklore. Her idea for Moira's name had come from that. She hesitated over it and then looked further. She didn't want to name them for an immortal who might object to them using the name.

She pulled a couple of books out and sat cross-legged on the floor. The kittens and girls had occupied the couch and were getting reacquainted, which seemed to involve lots of wrestling. All that was missing was Coyote, who was still outside with Bes.

It seemed so surreal, here she was, sitting on the floor of a house built into a Monster's skull, waiting to be taken to safety while the end of the world was coming. And she was looking up a name for an immortal being who was currently shaped like a kitten. A rather large and inquisitive kitten, she thought as he romped over and leapt up on the book to headbutt at her face, rubbing his cheeks on hers.

She looked down at the book she had been leafing through. "How about Lancelot?" He chuffed a little sneeze. Linn chuckled... "Then maybe Gareth. He was one of the Knights of the Round Table, and the name is Welsh for peaceful."

Spot One put his paws on her shoulders and started to lick her face.

"Hey! That tickles... I'll take that as a yes. You're Gareth, now."

Patricia and Moira came over slowly, still walking unsteadily. Blackie walked between them, letting them hold onto him as they needed support. Physically they might look three years old, but they had only assumed a two-legged form three days before. It was harder to learn to walk with two than with four.

Linn hugged all of them as they got near enough, grabbing them in an indiscriminate group. She had thought she had lost them. Now, having them all near to her was making her cry, still, but happy tears now, and those she didn't mind. Blackie and Gareth wiggled free and prowled around the room, Patricia and Moira were content to snuggle a little longer.

Linn got up and gave them each a hand to hold onto. They walked across the room slowly and she put them each in a chair. Then she pointed at herself. "Linn. My name is Linn."

She pointed at Patricia "Pat. your name is Pat." and then at Moira, repeating the phrase with her own name. "Now you say it. I am..." she pointed at herself. The girls both giggled. Linn sighed. "I guess you guys will start talking when you are ready, huh."

They climbed down from their chairs and toddled off hand in hand. They didn't get far before their brothers pounced on them. Linn went back to clean up the books she had taken out. She stopped when she was done, running a finger along the spines of the library. She was beginning to have a feeling the science fiction collection was as much a part of the answers to immortals as the mythology books were.

Reluctantly, she turned away from the books and started to make dinner. Coyote's late breakfast for her was a distant memory. She looked in the vintage refrigerator with its avocado door and saw the leftover stew from the night before, and four fresh rabbit carcasses. She smiled. Chicken Fried Rabbit, coming up. With biscuits, and... something from the garden she had seen coming in. Not to mention that she'd been here thirty-six hours and hadn't been back outside.

She looked in the cupboard and found a colander. Carrying it, she opened the door and stepped outside. She looked down at the valley. Coming in that evening, she had been too tired for the weirdness of it all to truly hit her.

"Alice, you've fallen down the rabbit hole." She muttered to herself. A valley full of bones, mythical beings that might not be magical, and a mixed bag of toddlers and kittens. And she could see whatever it was that powered the immortals, and was having really weird dreams that might not be dreams.

She carefully did not focus on the power that rippled through the valley. One glimpse of that had been enough. Walking down the stairs, she could see Bes and Coyote walking with the horses near the mouth of the valley. She realized there was no fodder for the horses in the blackened valley. If Coyote was going to be gone for a while they needed to be somewhere they could eat.

She walked around the nose of the skull to where the little garden was. As she'd caught a glimpse of it before, she had thought it was raised beds, and it was, but the beds were made of yet more bones. She chuckled to herself. Coyote was nothing if not practical. There were green beans and cucumbers that needed harvested.

Once she had enough for them all, she headed back up the stairs, glad of the fresh air. She had no desire to roam around the eerie valley, though. She kept getting flashes of power out of the corner of her eyes, the umber of the dead monster more often than the green of Coyote.

Dinner prep while keeping an eye on the children kept her busy, until she heard footsteps on the stairs. Coyote came in first, the resemblance to his beast form acute as he raised his nose, sniffing audibly. He walked to the sink and washed his hands, looking at what she was doing.

"Look, Bes," he called jovially. "She has made us ambrosia!"

Linn laughed. "The secret must be in how hungry you are."

"I could eat a bear." The stocky god chimed in cheerfully.

Linn pulled another piece of rabbit from the skillet she was frying in and put it on the draining rack.

"Go ahead and start. I just need to finish up." She slid another piece into the sizzling fat. "You don't have any bigger pans." she told Coyote.

He shrugged. "I don't have company often. If you will come to cook, I will get a bigger pan."

Bes collected the little girls and put them on cushions so they could reach the table top. He fed them and himself until Linn sat down and took Patricia's bowl from him.

"You feed Moira." She told him.

"Moira?"

"We picked out names today. This is Moira..." She pointed at the black-haired toddler who had gone by Spot Two. "This is Patricia, or Patch..." She pointed at the redhead who looked up from the green bean she was playing with and smiled at all of them before going back to her amusement. Linn was sure she wasn't going to eat that green thing.

Linn leaned over and fished Spot One out from under the table into her lap, grunting slightly at the effort. He was easily twenty-five pounds already. "And this is now Gareth."

Bes smiled. "Good name."

The kitten inspected her plate and then looked up at her hopefully. Linn shook her head at him. "I don't think so. You've had yours." She put him down again.

"What about the big one?" Coyote asked, grinning at the byplay.

"He likes his name." Linn answered. "For now, at least. Blackie is a pretty stubborn kitten, aren't you?" She cooed at him. He came and sprawled next to her and she reached down to tickle his furry stomach.

"I will clean up tonight." Coyote announced. He patted his stomach. "Thank you, Linn, for the meal."

Bes nodded. "Thank you, child. You cook well."

Linn could feel herself blushing.

Bes stood. "I need to get my bedroll. Linn, I need you to relax and get some rest. We have a long way to go tomorrow."

Linn nodded. "I think I'll lie down with a book."

Coyote went over to the library and looked for a minute. He pulled out a worn hardcover with no dust jacket and handed it to her. "Try this one."

"Thank you." Linn looked at it curiously. She hadn't read it before.

She curled up on the couch and started the story. She looked up when Bes covered her with the afghan. He grinned at her. "Just like your mom."

Linn nodded and remembered that she needed to call her mother. "Can I call her?"

He shook his head. "No cell service here. You can call her tomorrow. Long drive to the airport."

"All right." She went back to the book. He laughed. Linn just read. Her mother used to tease her that the world could end and she wouldn't look up from the page.

19

GATHERING CHILDREN

From Idaho, Sekhmet and Steve returned to the high path and traveled south faster than they could have in a car or airplane. The featureless tunnel of the high path warped perceptions, and it was hard to see one another, but they could talk and did.

"The Shiwanna child first, and then what?" Steve asked.

"She's young, maybe five? So we will need to take her to Sanctuary and then go on to the next one."

"So, we are only bringing the young ones in... the children who have not yet matured."

"That's what I was thinking. I don't think we will get too much of an argument from parents. Although the Shiwanna can only loosely be called parents."

"This is true."

Sekhmet thought about this as they loped along in companionable silence. The Shiwanna were a group of immortals who had become Zuni gods of clouds and rain. They had pooled energy and created another one of them, as a human child, and were raising her in Colorado.

"What is it about humans," Sekhmet mused, "that makes us so optimistic?"

"That we risk having children?" Steve inquired.

"Yes. We know, of anyone, how terrible life can be. Yet we choose to continue, and to multiply."

"Not all of us continue. And the children... that's a new thing again."

She nodded, before remembering he couldn't see her. "Only in the last hundred years. It's been so many centuries... since the Old Ones first came to Earth. Children were common, then."

They fell, then, letting go of the high path and drifting to earth. Reforming, they ran on, the vision of people on the streets running over them like water. All mortals saw was what the god wanted them to see... which was nothing.

The Shiwanna lived on a small commune in New Mexico. Sekhmet and Steve paced up the dusty driveway, letting themselves be seen by the shy band of immortals. They were met at the door.

The tall, silver-haired woman spoke with the peculiar resonance of many voices coming from one mouth.

"Welcome. Enter, and refresh yourselves."

Sekhmet bowed her head, forehead to the packed earth floor. Steve did the same. Respect was an important part of the immortal's peculiar culture that had evolved over the centuries. Without it, wars could have raged out of control.

They followed their hostess into the courtyard, not seeing anyone else. She pointed to a low table, which held a platter of food and bowls of water.

"Partake, and the pool is at your service, as well."

She went back out through the door they had come in. Sekhmet and Steve looked at one another and shrugged.

"Might as well. With this heat, I'd love a dip in the pool." Steve walked into the water without further comment, paddling when it got deep enough and ducking his head under, letting the cool water roll through his glossy black fur. Sekhmet jumped in and splashed him joyously. Big cats, unlike their smaller domestic cousins, loved the water.

They both climbed out and shook in the courtyard garden. "At least they won't have to water the plants today." Sekhmet joked when they were done.

They ate, and drowsed in the sun, fur drying, waiting for their hosts to show themselves. Sekhmet lay next to Steve and rested her chin on his back.

"I didn't expect this." She commented.

"Me, neither." He stretched lazily, careful not to disturb her.

"A mini vacation. More relaxing in a couple hours than I've had in... I don't know how long."

"We should do this again."

Sekhmet lifted her head and looked at him. "What? Run around the world rescuing children?"

"No... take a day at the spa." He rolled over and licked her face. "We should build a house with a pool like this."

"How very... human. To live together in?" She eyed him dubiously. Steve was not exactly one to seek commitment.

"At least some of the time?" Now, that was more like him.

They were interrupted then by a solemn, big-eyed little girl dressed in a jumper and white blouse. She carried a little knapsack. She dropped an awkward little curtsey as they sat up and looked at her.

"Hello, my name is Cloud." She piped in a sweet, high voice.

"Hello, child." Sekhmet greeted her gravely.

"I am ready to go now."

They looked at each other. The Shiwanna were not normal, even by immortal standards. This self-assured little being was in keeping with their ways.

Steve crouched. "Climb aboard, Cloud."

She scrambled onto him, a small smile on her face. He stood and she clung to his fur.

"Ready?" Sekhmet asked.

The small child gave a little nod, and the three of them ran for the High Path, and sanctuary.

20

ON THE ROAD AGAIN

*P*acking two toddlers, the kittens, a teenager, and a burly Egyptian god into the truck was a chore. Linn held the toddlers and the kittens sat on her feet, mostly. By the time they pulled into Grangeville she was exhausted. Bes shot her a sympathetic look.

"Two more stops and then we get to the airport."

She stayed in the truck for the first stop, but at the second one, where they picked up the rented minivan, she sighed with relief as she buckled the girls into their new car seats. The kittens hopped in eagerly, and Linn climbed into the passenger seat.

"Get some sleep." Bes recommended.

Linn glared at him. "Are you going to make me?"

He chuckled. "No, just you had it worse than I did during the drive out."

She sighed. Trying to keep four wiggly children out of his way had been a challenge. "You have a point."

Leaning her chair back, she closed her eyes. She didn't awaken until Bes shook her shoulder. She sat up and looked around. They were in the rental parking lot at the airport.

"We're here." Bes told her.

She climbed out and opened the sliding door. The two kittens poured out and took up position on either side of her. Linn giggled.

"Look, they are guarding me."

Bes came around with Patricia. "Here, hold her."

Linn frowned at him. "Hey..."

Bes pulled Moira into his arms. "Come on, we're being met."

Lin juggled the little girl and her pack. She had put Lambent into the pack to avoid uncomfortable questions at the terminal. She had to trot to keep up with Bes.

"Where are we going?"

"Hawaii. Keep up."

"Hawaii?!" Linn squealed. Then she stopped. "What is wrong with you?"

Bes ignored her and pointed. "Look, there he is."

Linn spotted him immediately, the tall, dark man standing so still in the midst of the crowd. His power flared like a torch above him, iridescent waves of many colors.

"Bes, who is that?"

Bes hurried his steps, holding out his free hand to the tall Latin man. "Quetzalcoatl! You came yourself."

The Mayan god took the extended hand and pulled the shorter man closer, bending to kiss both his cheeks. "I had to meet my grandchildren." He kissed the top of Moira's head.

He took Linn's hand and kissed the back of it gently. "The brave protector of my children."

She blushed and handed him Pat and he started off, waving them to follow. "Come, come. I haven't much time."

The small group started through the terminal. Linn realized the people couldn't see them. The crowd just flowed around them like they weren't even there. She watched people walking and talking right past her as though she were invisible. The kittens were glued to her side, eyes wide. She felt weird about the whole thing. She had been isolated all summer, and had spent time fleeing through the woods ahead of angry gods. People made her feel jumpy and nervous now.

She was distracted by this for a moment, and then re-focused on Bes. Something was wrong. She sped up to catch up with him.

"Bes..." She started, just as they reached a nondescript door that Quetzalcoatl swept open and waved them through.

They stepped out directly onto the tarmac. Linn looked around for a second, stunned at the level of noise and activity. Then she scooped up the kittens. They were heavy for her to carry, but she was afraid they would run out into trouble. It was noisy enough she might not be able to call them back.

Quetzalcoatl led them to a small business jet and once they were all in, pushed the button to retract the stairs. "Make yourself comfortable," he bid them affably. "But buckle up, we have a hot take off." He went into the tiny cabin

Bes and Linn buckled in the toddlers. As Linn turned from strapping Moira into a chair that looked more like an overstuffed recliner, she saw that Bes had already strapped in and had his eyes closed. She went and sat beside him, buckling in. She laid her hand on top of his.

He turned and looked at her, smiling faintly. He took her hand in his and then closed his eyes again.

"You're afraid of flying." She stated firmly, sure of what she was saying.

He hesitated before responding. "Yes, I am."

"You're an immortal."

He looked at her again. "Yes, I am, but we still have fears. Do you think the Old Ones would be trying to end civilization as we know it if they weren't afraid?"

"You don't have to fly."

He grunted. Linn thought it might have been one of his belly laughs under other circumstances. "I wasn't going to try to walk the high path with four babies and you, child."

He closed his eyes again. Linn felt the shudder as the plane broke the bonds of Earth and leapt into the sky. He tightened his grip on her hand momentarily, and then pulled it away.

"Bes?"

"Yes, Linn?"

"Have you ever had your own children?"

He looked at her again, and she couldn't see a trace of power flickering in his eyes for once. They were just dark and sad.

"No, I haven't."

"Oh." Linn wasn't sure what else to say, so she took his hand again, feeling the leathery calluses and the strength in it.

She looked around the cabin, at the kittens, sprawled on the soft carpet, asleep already. The twins were already drooping, half asleep. This was so different from the last plane she had been on, where all she was worried about was dieting and being able to access the 'net. She looked down at herself. Curves intact, but to be honest, it seemed so unimportant now.

She wondered what was going to happen next. Her adventure was over, it seemed. She was flying off to be a glorified babysitter. With Bes, and this Sanctuary they had been mentioning, she was going to be redundant. She sighed. The kittens were safe, that was what mattered.

She unbuckled and went forward to the cockpit. "May I come in?" she asked softly.

Quetzalcoatl looked around at her, smiling. "Of course."

She slid into the empty co-pilot's seat and looked out the window. Mountains below them, still. "I love the view from up here."

"Bes asleep?" He looked concerned, and she realized he knew how Bes felt about flying.

She nodded. "He did this for me, didn't he?"

"Yes, he didn't want you to have to travel alone."

"Do you know why he doesn't have children?"

Quetzalcoatl looked startled. He twisted around in his chair to face her directly. "In a way, he does. He raised many immortal children, you know. He considers two of them his in all but blood. He's in the background, but in a very important way."

"I've gathered that. That's why Grampa called him to be our babysitter."

He nodded. Unlike most immortals, who were fully human or fully beast, that she had seen, his eyes were large, golden serpent eyes. He blinked, slowly.

"He is patient beyond most immortals' reckoning. For all our timelessness, few of us are known for our foresight. Even your grandfather was reckless, in his time."

"I've been doing a lot of reading all summer. Trying to figure out... what you are."

He chuckled. "Smart girl and brave."

"Well, Grampa said you aren't gods, but he can't... won't tell me what you really are."

"Neither can I, child," he said gently.

Linn nodded. "I know that and am not asking. I think I can figure it out on my own."

He laughed. "I really can't wait until you meet the Scholar, the two of you should be... formidable."

"The Scholar?"

"Hypatia of Alexandria."

Linn felt her eyes widen. "Really? The librarian... I didn't know she was an immortal."

"Not many did. She always eschewed power. Her talents lay in connecting the pieces of a puzzle. Which is why your grandfather has recruited her mind in our struggle against the power-mad ones who would destroy our home."

"And I get to meet her?"

He laughed again. "Indeed, and I think she will be as charmed as I am."

Linn felt her cheeks blush. "I think I'll go back and read for a while. Can I bring you anything?"

"Once we are over the ocean I can walk around a little, I'll get it then."

Linn went back to the cabin. Bes was awake, the children were all asleep.

"Hey." She grabbed her pack and sat down with him again. "Coyote loaned me some books. I mean... I think he gave them to me. I don't know when I'll see him again. But he said it was a loan."

"You'll see him again. He likes you." Bes reassured her.

"Do you want one to read?" Linn realized as she said this that she'd never actually seen him read.

"Yes, please."

Linn pulled the books out and offered them to him. He gave a subdued chuckle as he looked at them. "Quite an interesting collection."

"He picked them out and said I should read them."

"I've read this one." He handed the book she had been reading the night before back to her.

"I'm enjoying it." she told him. "I hadn't read any of them."

"I'll keep this one. The author writes a good, fast story." He showed her the newest one, which still had its dust jacket. A rearing golden dragon appeared behind a woman dressed scantily and carrying a bow and arrow. Linn eyed it.

"What is she supposed to be?"

"Wood elf, I think."

"Oh." She opened her book and then looked back at him. "Bes? Are there..."

"Elves and fairies?" He filled in with a smile.

"Yeah."

"Well, sort of. Some immortals have chosen to live differently."

Linn blinked. Her world kept turning further upside down. She went back to her book.

They were both quietly reading when Quetzalcoatl came back to the cabin.

"Ah, noses in books together, I see. Care for a sandwich and a soda?"

Linn got up and helped him with them. She didn't think Bes was going to get out of his seat while they were in the air. She brought him food and drink, which he eyed dubiously but ate obediently.

"Feels strange to be taking care of you." She commented, sitting back down with him.

"Feels strange to be taken care of."

"Well, someone has to do it." She shot back tartly.

This sally did provoke a laugh out of him. "Child, I am older than the human race. You are still a child."

"I'm human. We grow fast."

He snorted. "Feed the children."

He was asleep, or at least faking it well, when she was done taking care of the kittens and toddlers. The tiny galley had been messy after dinner, making her glad she'd chosen to feed them in there. Blackie and Gareth used their improvised litter pan. Altogether, when she was done and cleaned up, it had been quite a while.

With the kids settled, she sat back down and took his hand in hers again. Then she closed her eyes and fell asleep. She hadn't dreamed for days, but she woke up shaking, from the dream about running through the fog with Blackie, Lambent held high, a beacon in the night. For the first time, she heard a sound. A bull-throated roar she knew was Bes... She angled toward it, tripped over something yielding, and fell... fell...

Linn sat bolt upright with a little squeak. The cabin lights had been turned down, and it was all but dark. Bes was snoring softly. The children were all asleep.

She stood and stretched out some of the kinks. Going forward to the cockpit, she rapped on the lintel of the open door.

"Come in, child."

"Thanks. I wanted a little company."

He smiled, a flash of white teeth in the dim lights from the instruments.

"Couldn't sleep?"

"I had a dream." Linn told him, looking out the windows at the stars. "I know Grampa said immortals aren't magical. But the Oracles at Delphi... prophecy is a recurrent theme throughout mythology. And I keep having this same dream."

"Ah." Linn inferred an unseen nod. "You are correct, there are those who have the power to foresee. It is rare for it to be clear."

Linn sighed. "I kinda figured that."

"What have you been dreaming about?" Quetzalcoatl asked her gently.

"I'm walking in a fog, using Lambent as a torch."

"Lambent?"

"The sword Grandpa made me. I named her Lambent because that's what she is... she's softly brilliant with flickers of power."

"You have the Sight?"

"Yes. You are a lot of colors, Bes is just... white. Grampa is lava-flow colored. Coyote is grass green. But what's really weird is that I could see the power of the dead monster in Coyote's valley."

"Really? I have never been there."

"Can all immortals see power?"

"No, not all. Some of us can."

Linn fell silent, thinking about this. She still wasn't sure what her sight could do for her. It was pretty, she thought now that she'd gotten over her initial fear of it.

Quietly, Quetzalcoatl asked. "And the rest of your dream?"

"Oh... well, Blackie is with me, only he's big. Big enough I can rest my hand on his head." She cupped her hand in the air, showing him how tall, while her skin glowed red in the instrument lights. "We're running. I put Lambent down by my side after a while... I think it's lighter. Then I trip over something... something soft and I fall. I fall into a hole, I think."

"Does it change?"

Linn hesitated. "Well, tonight, I could hear Bes. He was... well, it was like a war cry."

"He does that." the Mayan god murmured.

"So I was trying to get to him. Only I tripped."

"And fell in a hole?"

"Well, I just kept falling, past where I thought I should have hit the ground."

"Linnaea, I can't tell you if it is a dream, or a foretelling. I wish I could. The future without uncertainty would certainly be easier."

"Yes." Linn wasn't sure how she felt about that, but she felt better for having told someone about it.

"What do you want to be when you grow up?'

"What?" Linn was confused by the change in topics. "Oh... Well, I wanted to be a teacher."

"An honorable profession."

"Right now, I'm not sure, though."

"You come by that naturally." He smiled again. "Your mother is a notable adventure seeker."

"I hadn't thought of it that way." Linn got up. "I'm going to try and get some rest."

"Good idea. Sleep when you can."

She sighed. "That's what Grampa said."

Linn went back into the darkened cabin. The children were still asleep. Bes turned his head and opened his eyes briefly. She sat down next to him and took his hand without speaking. He squeezed her fingers and then she closed her eyes. This time, she didn't dream.

2 1

GATHERING IN

Sekhmet sighed and stretched. They had run halfway around the globe and weren't done yet. They had Cloud safe, and the Japanese triplets, who had been a handful to retrieve. Their next charge was the oldest of the children on the list. He wouldn't have been on the list at all, but his mother had insisted. With her people scattered and her legends all but forgotten she felt vulnerable.

Sedna, the mistress of the Inuit underworld had a thirteen-year-old son, whose father she had not named. Raised on the edges of human society, in the last frontier, he was likely to be another interesting child, Sekhmet mused.

They fell to Earth near the designated meeting place. The tundra was ablaze with fall color, the end of the warm season came early here. They walked carefully through the bright clumps of blueberries and birches, none of them came higher than Sekhmet's knees.

A bright-eyed Siberian husky came bouncing up to them, barking. Sekhmet laughed. "Hello, Stith."

The dog transformed to a short, stocky boy with a beaming smile. "Hello! You must be Sekhmet, and you must be the Mayan god of Terrestrial Fire."

"I prefer Steve. Nice to meet you, young man." The black jaguar laughed.

"Boy, am I glad you guys are here for me!"

"Has something happened here?" Sekhmet looked around, pricking her ears forward.

"No, nothing has EVER happened here!" Stith scowled. "Mom won't let me go to Anchorage. I can't have a ski-doo. I am dying to get out of here."

Steve laughed. "Well, then, let's get going, kid."

The two great cats exchanged amused glances as Stith picked up a backpack. This one was normal as American apple pie. He ran the high path with them exuberantly.

At the Sanctuary, one of the coblyn greeted them with a bow, and a lei for the delighted Stith. The goblin turned from the boy to Sekhmet. "Linn and the kittens will land shortly. Would you like to wait for them?"

Sekhmet sighed and rubbed her face along the soft inner side of her foreleg. "We still have three children to bring back, and they are on the other side of the world."

"No, they aren't." The coblyn contradicted her.

"What?" She wasn't sure she'd heard that right, and cocked her ears at him.

"We are flying them in. Cora is on a private jet of her father's, and the twins are flying commercial with their mother."

"Why not wait for us?"

"Heff didn't want you two to be exhausted, and there have been no moves made against the other children."

Sekhmet sat and sighed. "And might not be. But I do feel better knowing they are all safe."

"Heff said you would say that. He also said to tell you that he could give you guys three days, but then you had to be at HQ with him."

Steve laughed. "Sounds like him. Well, I know these sore paws could use a break."

"Shall we go to the airport?"

"Absolutely. Let's go get the kids, then we can play on the beach for a while."

She laughed at him. "I thought your feet were sore."

"I'm a god." He shrugged. "I can heal them."

She batted at him with a paw the size of a dinner plate and he ducked away, laughing. She chased for a minute, and then they returned to Stith. "Are you going to be all right?" Sekhmet asked him.

"Can I go to the beach, too?"

"Yep, you can meet us there, right?" She looked at the coblyn, who nodded.

"Of course." He assured the Inuit boy.

"Why not all the kids and we'll make it a welcome party. When are the others due in?"

"Cora should be here in a few hours. The others, not until tomorrow." The coblyn looked like he was getting into the idea.

"See if you can coax the Scholar out in the sun a little, too?" Steve suggested.

"Quetzalcoatl thought she and Linn should meet."

"Oh, really?" Sekhmet mused. "Yes, I think that's a great idea."

She and Steve nodded to the boy and his guide and started for the front entrance. The winding tunnels of the Sanctuary contained a lot of things no one on the surface of the island had any idea about. The Library was only one of them. It made getting from one place to another tedious, but they still had time.

Sekhmet walked shoulder to shoulder with Steve, feeling relaxed in knowing that they were done with their mission, and the kittens were coming here. No one knew how long this war would last, and Hawaii certainly wasn't a place to be stranded should civilization come to screeching halt. For now, and the children, it was a good place. Pele's power so saturated the islands that the Old Ones didn't dare approach.

22

HOMECOMING

*L*inn jolted awake as the plane touched down. She reached down, but the buckle was done. Looking across the cabin, she could see the twins were holding hands and looking around with wide eyes. Bes was sitting still, holding onto both the armrests. She knew without asking he would do this until they touched down. Blackie and Gareth were nowhere in sight.

"Blackie, Gareth?" she called.

Quetzalcoatl answered. "With me, Linn. Don't worry."

Linn sighed and leaned back. Her protectorship might be coming to an end, but she thought she would always feel like this toward all the kittens. The plane slowed and then turned. She felt a little sad. Her adventures were done. Pretty soon she would probably get on a plane back to Seattle and the apartment.

When the plane stopped, she unbuckled the girls, giving them an extra hug and kiss as she did so. Gareth came scampering into the cabin, his tail held high. Quetzalcoatl, laughing, followed him.

"They watched the landing from the co-pilot's seat. Blackie is still glued to it. Also, you have a greeting party waiting for you."

"Oh, Blackie!" Linn handed the girls off to Bes, who put them down and took their hands.

She went into the cockpit, where Blackie had his paws up on the instrument panel and was lashing his tail.

"Looks like fun, doesn't it? Maybe you can be a pilot someday like Quetzalcoatl."

He turned and looked at her, and for the first time she saw his power in his eyes. Raging blue fire... she blinked.

"You're excited, but you can't stay here." she told him firmly. He hopped down and came over to her, putting his forepaws on her knees and headbutting her stomach. "I'm staying with you, my friend." Linn assured him.

They followed Bes and the twins out of the plane and down the narrow steps. A small group of people was waiting for them there in the bright sunlight. Linn squinted, trying to see. Bes handed the girls off to a tall man... Steve, she realized. Gareth and Blackie ran ahead of her and pounced on their mother, who sat down on the tarmac with an exaggerated "Oof!" before ruffling their fur and letting them lick her face.

Linn smiled, and then got a good look at the other woman.

"Grandmother!" she shrieked, and ran into her arms. As they closed tightly around her, she could feel tears rising in her eyes. Grandma smelled the same as ever... exotic and flowery. "I missed you so much." Linn told her, choking up.

"I missed you too." Her grandmother put a hand under her chin and tilted her head back. "Let me look at you, how much you've grown!"

Linn gasped. Her grandmother's eyes glowed with power. Rich crimson and white danced with yellow glints. "You are Pele..."

Her grandmother's round cheeks appled with the broadness of her grin. "Yes, I am. Welcome to my home, my dear."

Linn laughed in delight. "Of course, he would choose you." She marveled. It seemed so obvious now.

"Maybe it was me who chose him! Pursued him shamelessly, too!" The older woman retorted joyfully.

They both laughed, hugging again. When they finally let go and turned to look at Bes, still arm in arm, he chuckled.

"Anyone seeing the two of you together would know you were related.

Although," he made a small bow in Pele's direction. "As mother and daughter, not Grandmother."

Pele laughed heartily. "Flattery will get you everywhere, Bes. How are you, old war-horse?"

"Well, despite the harrowing experience of having trained Linn." He returned smoothly with a wink at Linn, who stuck her tongue out at him.

"Do you stay with us?" Pele asked.

Linn looked at her in dismay. It hadn't occurred to her that Bes would leave them once he'd brought them to Sanctuary. She turned and looked at him and knew what he would say before the words left his lips.

"No, I return to Heff. I am needed, he tells me, the battle is coming faster than expected."

Linn went to him, feeling her lip trembling, but not wanting to cry. He hugged her gently. "You will be safe, child."

"I'll miss you. Will I ever see you again?"

"Of course. I need to do this, though. Don't change while I'm gone?"

"I hadn't planned to."

He chucked her chin and hugged Pele, who whispered something in his ear. He nodded and then walked away, around the plane. Linn's vision was blurry with tears. She gulped. "Now what, Grandma?"

Pele squeezed her hand gently. "Now we go home."

Linn looked around. Quetzalcoatl was standing, waiting for her. Steve and Sekhmet, still in human form, were walking the children toward waiting cars.

"Thank you for bringing us." Linn told the Mayan god. "I guess we are safe now."

"You are, child. Don't grieve. He always keeps his word."

"It's just..." She felt her voice slide away. She cleared her throat. "Give my love to Grampa Heff."

"Of course, I will."

"And mine." Pele added. Quetzalcoatl laughed.

"I think it will be safer for me if you do that yourself, my Lady."

Linn watched him walk up the stairs, and then turned to follow her grandmother to the car. She settled into the backseat with her grandmother and Blackie, who had chosen to ride with them. The driver, who looked very small to Linn's eyes, nodded to Pele and pulled out once they were settled.

"Now," Pele turned to Linn and took the girl's hands in hers. "Tell me everything."

Linn giggled a little, her laughter finally banishing her tears, although there was still a knot in her chest. "Well, I thought it was just going to be another boring summer at Grampa Heff's cabin... He doesn't have internet or anything!"

Her tale took them all the way to the entrance of the Sanctuary, a surprisingly normal door in an office building, which led to an elevator. They all crowded in, Sekhmet adding a few comments as she realized what Linn was telling her grandmother. Linn picked up Moira and balanced her on her hip without even thinking about it, not realizing until later it was not something the Linn from the beginning of this summer would have done. She had despised babysitting. The kittens had been different... cute, cuddly, and helpless.

Linn kissed Moira's head and told her grandmother about the helpless flight through the forest, thinking the girls were dead in the wreckage of the cabin. The toddler hugged her neck.

"Linn!" she said clearly. They all fell silent and stared at the little girl. She giggled. "Linn!" she said again, obviously pleased to be the center of attention. The elevator doors slid open.

Pat, not to be outdone by her dark-haired sister, pointed. "Go!"

They all laughed and stepped out into the brightly lit tunnel. Linn looked around her in amazement. The tunnel stretched off in either direction, with doors every so often. Her grandmother spoke softly. "I got the idea from the cold war of the humans. I wanted to create a place where some of us could be safe through almost anything."

"What about regular people?"

"We are doing our best, child. But for them to be safe, there must be guardians, and the guardians must have sanctuary."

Linn nodded. That made sense. She knew her grandfather and grandmother both wanted humanity to continue to grow, unchecked. It was almost, she mused, as though they, Bes, Coyote, and even Quetzalcoatl, felt about humans the way they felt about children. Her train of thought was interrupted as a small train of... golf carts? that pulled up to them.

A funny little person with large ears hopped out of the first once and gave them all a sweeping bow. "Welcome, welcome!" he cried in a squeaky voice.

Then the other drivers all crowded around them, putting leis on Linn and the children. Pele laughed. "They all wanted to come to the airport to greet you, but it was decided such a crowd would be too much to hide."

Pele and the lead driver, who Linn had decided was the leader of the little people came over to her. Behind them, Linn could see the little people, who had a greenish tinge to their skin and points on their ears, making much of the kittens and little girls. They were getting into the carts with their parents.

"Linn, this is Daffyd. He is the king of the coblyns."

Linn took his offered hand and tried to curtsey. "Pleased to meet you, sir, um... majesty?"

He laughed, a bright chortle. "Daffy is fine. 'Tis what Pele calls me."

"And you are all... coblyns?" Linn was trying to remember where she'd read that word.

"Aye, also known as goblins and the little people. When Pele opened the Sanctuary she called in a gang of us to help with design and construction." He shrugged. "We liked it so much we asked to stay on." He waved her to the nearest car. "Come, then! We want to get you to your rooms, and then tonight we party!"

Linn climbed in the cart with her grandmother, and looked around as they whizzed down the tunnel. Grandma murmured in her ear "The coblyns modified the carts. Keep your hands inside, dear, we are going faster than we ought to."

Linn nodded. She was not inclined to let so much as a finger stray. "How long is the tunnel?"

"Oh, I don't really know. The coblyns add to it every so often. With my power, it's not going to collapse, and they really are superior miners, you know. Many miles, that's for sure."

"Wow. And a party?"

"Oh, yes. We wanted to welcome all the children here with a party on the beach. It was decided we would give you a few hours to rest, and then have our little luau. Linn..." Pele hugged her close. "I am so happy you are finally here."

Linn snuggled back. "How many of us are there?"

"Well, you aren't really one of the children. Only those who haven't reached maturity yet were brought here."

Linn felt absurdly pleased. She wasn't a child.

Her grandmother continued. "So, let's see. There is Cloud, who is very quiet, and about six years old. Stith, from the Arctic, is 13 and the happiest boy. The Japanese triplets, Akako, Botan, and Cho are very energetic. They are seven years old. Cora will be here shortly, she is Hades' daughter, and I was told she is twelve. And then in the morning Parja and Fjorgg from Lithuania will be the last arrivals. They are twins, nine years old."

"So, with the kittens, there are twelve children."

"Yes, and it should be a lot of fun for all of you to get to know one another."

Linn nodded dubiously. "The kittens are babies compared to the rest."

"Not really. They are maturing like cats... the girls are about three, and the boys perhaps even older than that. The girls will mature at a more human rate now that they have chosen this form."

"I would have thought immortals would mature at a slower rate than humans."

"Not and survive among humanity."

"What happens to immortals that don't make it?"

Pele started to answer, but they stopped just then. Daffyd hopped out and opened the double doors. Pele followed him through them. Linn walked into what looked like a huge living room, with flowering plants and waterfalls everywhere.

"Welcome home, dear." Pele kissed her cheek.

Blackie padded with her as Daffyd led them down a hall. "Here is your room, Linnaea."

"Call me Linn, please."

"Gladly!" the little creature beamed at her. "Now, you have a few hours. There is food and drink within for you."

He bowed and went out again, leaving Linn to look around the room.

She was suddenly very tired, and homesick. It was a nice room, a bit like a hotel room. Bland, she decided. Blackie leaned on her leg.

"We've come a long way from the hayloft."

She started to pick him up and then decided against it. He was really too old to baby. He hopped up on the bed and sprawled out, purring.

"I miss it." She told him, even though he didn't look like he was listening.

She went into the bathroom, which didn't resemble a hotel bathroom at all. A big tub made her decide to take a bath. She hadn't been able to do that since she had left home. She started the water running and went back out into the other room.

"Shoot. I don't know where my clothes are." Her pack, with Lambent neglected in it, lay on the floor. She pulled Lambent out of it, and then unsheathed her. The dancing fire, red and white with little tendrils of her own pink, made her remember the bonding with Bes and Grandpa.

"I hope they are ok." She whispered, sliding Lambent back away.

She looked in the pack again. Her survival kit, looking rather useless in these surroundings, the books Coyote had given her. No clothes. She laughed suddenly, looking down at herself. She was going to a Hawaiian beach party dressed in ratty jeans, black t-shirt, and a flannel shirt two sizes too big.

"Oh, kitten. I never meant to be this much of a tomboy."

Blackie slitted one golden eye at her and then pointedly went back to sleep.

"I know you don't care." Linn threw one of her dirty socks at him. Those she had spares for in the survival kit, not that she needed them in Hawaii. Bath first, then she would try to figure it out. Maybe she could cut off the jeans and modify the tee to be cooler.

She soaked until her fingertips were pruny. Emerging from the bath wrapped in one towel with the other twisted around her long black hair, she felt positively decadent. She had decided to make her jeans into shorts, with their various rips they were ready for it anyway. If she cut the tee a little, sleeves off and cropped, maybe, it would work.

She stopped dead when she saw the room. Her pack was gone, Blackie and Lambent where she had left them. There was art on the walls, flowers in vases, and a bookcase on the far wall. It was filled. Open mouthed, Linn wandered over to it. She spotted Coyote's books, and a mix of her childhood favorites. She pulled a copy of the White Dragon off the shelf and realized it was her own copy. The inscription from her mother to her on her eighth birthday was on the flyleaf. Bewildered, she put it back.

Crossing the room again to the dresser, she pulled open the top drawer and found her underwear. Looking through it, she saw that some was her own, some was new. She started to dress with relief. She really, really hadn't wanted to put the dirty clothes back on. She stopped and looked around. It was gone, too.

Linn pulled a long, well-worn tee shirt on and looked at the clock. If she napped for an hour she'd have plenty of time. She curled up and the bed and pulled Blackie closer. He started to purr and she closed her eyes. She slept dreamlessly until the alarm she had set sounded.

23

BEACH PARTY

*L*inn got up and looked in the closet. She had no idea what to wear, but when she saw the dress hanging by itself, she guessed that it was the one. A vibrant blue covered with white hibiscus flowers, she realized as she took it off the hanger that it was a tankini and a wrap-around skirt. She was almost completely covered with it on, but it felt light and cool. She shook Blackie awake.

"You don't have to get dressed, but I know you're going to want to come play."

He stretched, showing his white fangs. "My, what long teeth you have." Linn teased him. He ignored her and trotted to the door. She opened it and they stepped out into the living room. Sekhmet and Steve, both back in great cat form, were lolling on the carpet. The girls were dressed in identical bright pink muumuus, and they ran to Linn when they saw her, hugging her tightly.

"Hey!" she bent and cuddled them, saying softly, "I didn't go anywhere."

Gareth strolled over nonchalantly, then reared up to lick her cheek. Linn wasn't fooled by his little-boy bravado. She rubbed his ears. "It's ok, I'm here."

She looked sheepishly at Sekhmet, who laughed. "They have known you longer than they have known me at this point, child. Don't worry. All will return to normal in time, but you..." She walked over to Linn, and then sat, face to face with the girl. "You will always be part of our family, and loved."

Sekhmet touched her cool, wet nose to Linn's, and then licked her cheek with the great rough tongue. Linn put her arms around the shaggy neck of the goddess. "Thank you." she whispered in the fur. "I have gained so much this summer."

"The same goes for me." Steve said gravely. He was sitting next to Sekhmet now. "You have only to call and I will come running."

Linn hugged him, too. His fur was sleeker, but the bulk of his musculature made him look as big as Sekhmet.

"Don't cry, Child. It's time to go party a little!" He laughed at her, showing his fangs off a little. They were very white against his gleaming black fur.

She chuckled. Moira took her hand. "Linn! Look!"

Linn followed the insistent little girl to a balcony she hadn't realized was there, it blended with the plants inside so well. The glass doors stood open, allowing the sea breeze to sweep into the room. She stood on the brink for a moment, smelling the familiar sea, and yet subtly different from the cold Pacific she had grown up with.

With Patch tugging on one hand and Moira on the other, she went down the path to the private beach, surrounded by cliffs on the land side. A perfect semi-circle of black sand, gleaming in torchlight as the setting sun flamed in reds and oranges over one cliff.

She could smell barbecue and hear laughter as they reached the beach. Blackie and Gareth raced past her, toward the waves. Patch and Moira giggled and took off after them. Linn followed, concerned for the little girls in the waves. Then she stopped as a foam-white woman rose up out of the waves and caught up Moira, who shrieked with giggles as several others emerged from the waves and started to play with the children.

Linn realized they must be Naiads, there to protect the children, and went back up the beach to where the adults had gathered. Pele met her and hugged her.

"I see you found your things."

"Yes, thank you. I was wondering what I was going to wear! The dress is pretty, thank you. How did you get my books here?"

"Come meet Cora, she's just arrived." Her grandmother didn't reply directly, and Linn let it go.

Linn followed her grandmother to where the slim, pale girl was standing and looking awkward. Linn felt badly for her. Taken from her family and brought to a strange place, even if it was a beautiful, comfortable place. At least Linn had family with her almost the whole time. And had made more family during the summer, too.

Linn held both her hands out to the younger girl. "You must be Cora, I'm Linn."

"Hullo." Cora smiled and took her hands. "Yes, I am. I've heard so much about you."

Linn blinked in surprise. "You have?"

"Of course. My father knows your father."

"What?" Linn squeaked.

"He sends his love." Cora went on, smiling more widely at Linn's reaction.

"Have you met him?"

"Oh, yes, I live with my father part of the year. The rest of the year I live in London with my mum."

Cora tucked Linn's arm in hers and they started to walk down the beach together. Linn was stunned and then the questions tumbled out of her as Cora answered cheerfully.

SEKHMET CAME to stand next to Pele. "Looks like they hit it off."

"Yes, I thought they might. Nothing in common, of course, but they are of an age, and have no peers here." the fiery goddess smiled at her friend.

"Stith and the kitsune have joined the furball in the surf." The cat woman looked toward the water, luminescent with the torchlight and a bioluminescent something the Naiads were providing. It was certainly very pretty.

Pele laughed. "Good, all the little furry children playing together."

"Botan is somewhere around here with Cloud. They are much alike."

"Very quiet and wise beyond their years. Not too much of a surprise."

"Steve and I head out tomorrow afternoon."

"Not going to wait?" Pele looked at her, a little surprised that they would cut their rest short.

Sekhmet shook her head. "I have a bad feeling about this."

Pele sighed. "I am afraid I agree with you. Something is going on. This is so unlike their past campaigns."

Sekhmet sipped from her glass. She was in human form for the party. Some things weren't possible with paws. Long stemmed glasses were one of them. Dresses were another, and a rare pleasure for her. She turned to look for Steve, who was helping a pair of coblyns with the grill.

"So predictably male." She murmured in amusement. Charred meat and fire, too, were peculiarly his milieu.

A running coblyn caught her attention. Pele and Steve saw him coming, too, and they all converged on the little man. "Plane... The plane went down."

"What!"

Pele cried out. "The twins, they went after the twins!"

Sekhmet turned to her. "Steve and I are going now." Her urgency made her voice rough.

"I am coming with you. Hypatia..." Pele looked around for the Scholar.

"I'm here." A voice came from the depths of a cushioned wicker chair. "I can keep an eye on the children."

"Thank you. Tell Linn where we went, please." Pele asked. The old woman stood, shedding some of her facade and moving more quickly than her normal.

"Go. I will take care of them."

They went, straight onto the High Path so quickly that none of the children realized they were gone until later.

24

HYPATIA

*L*inn and Cora had gone into the water, splashing and playing in the warm surf with the little kids. The kitsune, Linn learned, were the fox forms of the Japanese immortals. They were mischievous little girls. She hadn't met Botan or Cloud, yet. Stith, a blue-eyed husky in dog form, and every bit as gangly and happy as a boy, was a joyful addition.

Linn finally left the water, tired out, and walked up to the patio area where she had left her skirt. She didn't see anyone at first, until someone sitting in a shadowy chair cleared their throat.

"You must be Linn." A papery voice addressed her.

"Yes, ma'am." She walked curiously toward the chair until she could see a thin, elderly woman, her face a lacework of wrinkles framed by silver hair.

"Oh, call me Tia. Your grandmother, Sekhmet and Steve were called away."

"Oh." Linn felt her heart sink down to her toes. She swallowed to get the lump out of her throat.

"Yes, child. It isn't good. I will let Pele tell you when she returns." The scholar's voice was warmly sympathetic.

Linn thought for a moment. It couldn't be a crisis, or they would be bringing the children in. She finally spoke again, "I have been wanting to meet you, Tia."

"Oh, have you now?" The old lady smiled broadly.

"I have some questions I'd like to ask you... You might not be able to answer, but I need to talk to someone!" Linn burst out.

Hypatia laughed. "Tomorrow, then, we shall meet in the library. Tonight, I think you and I have our hands full with the children."

"I'm so glad we have the coblyns and the Naiads helping." Linn smiled at the coblyn who was managing the grill and he grinned back. Suddenly it clicked what they reminded her of. She covered her mouth and choked back her laugh into a coughing fit.

"What?" Hypatia leaned forward, smiling.

Linn leaned down and whispered. "I just realized, it's like living with Yoda's family..."

Hypatia looked blank. "Who?"

"Have you ever seen Star Wars?"

The old woman shook her head.

Linn settled into the chair next to her. "I wonder if the library has DVD's."

"Yes, there are quite a few. I haven't had time for them."

"Well, I think you and I should take a little time." Linn grinned. This would be fun.

Hypatia laughed again. "Child, you are a jewel."

Linn's stomach growled. "Oooh... the food smells good. I wonder if it's time to gather the kids?"

Daffyd appeared at her elbow, startling her. "They will come up when they are hungry, which should be about... now!"

Linn laughed as Blackie, dripping wet, led the charge to the picnic tables that had been set for the children. She excused herself from Hypatia, who seemed disinclined to get up, and went to help with serving.

The party wound down after dinner, as children started to get sleepy. coblyns who Linn hadn't met yet came and went, nodding and smiling at her but rarely speaking. Each sleepy child went off with one, until finally Linn and Hypatia were alone on the terrace.

"You should get some sleep, child."

"I'm waiting for my grandmother." Linn felt the weariness pulling her down, but didn't think she would be able to sleep until she knew what was going on.

"I don't think they will be back quickly, dear." Hypatia stood slowly and laid a hand on Linn's shoulder. "I'm going in. Why don't you try at least."

"All right." Linn nodded and got up, yawning as she did so. "I guess I should. Seems strange not to have to take care of the kittens."

Hypatia squeezed her hand. "Sleep well, dear."

"And you... I'll see you in the morning?"

"Yes, I'll be in the common room for breakfast."

Linn didn't know what time that would be, and decided she would find and ask a Coblyn before bed. "Ok."

Linn made her way up the path, missing her shadow kittens as she did. She wondered where they were. When she walked into her room, she found out... lying on her bed, fast asleep. She laughed.

"Good thing Grandma gave me a big bed." she told the sleeping furball.

After a shower and putting on jammies, Linn pushed Gareth out of the way and curled up, thinking about the evening. She thought she was going to be awake for a while... and then she drifted off.

Blackie sitting on her chest washing her face awakened her.

"Pthhh! Hey! Gettoffa me!" Linn rolled off the bed and landed with a thump on the floor. She glared up at the kitten, who was now lying on the bed looking down at her. He stuck a paw out and batted at her hair playfully.

"Oh, that's it..." Linn grabbed him and rolled him on his back, growling and tickling his stomach. He growled back and wrapped all four paws around her arm, engulfing her hand in his jaws. He didn't bite or scratch her, though. The kittens knew they could hurt, and chose not to. Gareth joined in the fray and the three of them wrestled for a few minutes.

Linn slipped away as the brothers played with one another. Dressing quickly, she ran a brush through her hair, wincing as the snarls from swimming pulled. Next time she needed to remember to braid it first. Leaving it in loose tendrils down her back, she slid on sandals and headed for breakfast.

147

Hypatia waved at her as she entered the big room where most meals were served. A coblyn greeted her at the door with a little bow.

"If you would tell me what you would like, it will be brought to you, Miss Vulkane."

Linn blinked. She didn't think anyone had ever called her that. "Can you call me Linn, please? I'd like ham and eggs if that's ok."

"Yes, we would be happy to call you Linn. And it will be out shortly."

Linn made her way through the scattered tables, water gardens and plants until she reached Hypatia. "It is so pretty in here."

"Very soothing and peaceful." Hypatia stood and kissed Linn's cheek. "Did you sleep well, child?"

"Yes, until the kittens woke me. Did Grandmother come home yet?"

"No," Hypatia shook her head and sat back down. "She sent word that it is complicated, and she will be home possibly tomorrow or the next day."

"Oh." Linn sat. "I'm feeling rather... lost. I don't know what to do with myself. The coblyns have the children well in hand..." To punctuate her point, a giggling Moira ran up.

"Linn!"

"Hey, sweety!" Linn scooped her up for a hug and nuzzled the little girl's neck. Moira squirmed to get down.

"Bye!" And she was off again, with a young Coblyn woman in pursuit.

"See?" Linn chuckled, turning back to the older woman, who was smiling at the cute display.

"Would you like to try your hand at being my research assistant?" Hypatia offered. Linn had no idea that she would be taking the place of Peter, who was caught on the High Plane and badly missed by his lover.

"Sure! I love to read and look stuff up. What do you need help with?"

"Your grandfather said you would probably be helpful. And then Sekhmet and Coyote, both told me the same thing."

"Wow." Linn was stunned at the references. "They said that?"

"Yes, dear, they all think highly of your intelligence, and your maturity. Your grandfather said you understand Operational Security, correct?"

Linn sobered. "Yes, ma'am. I know I wouldn't be able to talk to anyone about what we are doing."

Hypatia nodded. "Good girl. Now, as for what we are looking into, I will explain all in my office later. Now, please enjoy your breakfast."

Linn looked up to see a coblyn with a serving tray approaching.

"Hello, Linn!" the young woman said cheerfully. "I have your breakfast. When you're done, if you could bring your dishes to the pass through..." she pointed toward a set of double doors Linn guessed led to the kitchen. "Let me know if you need anything else! I'm Deirdre. I'm your guide here at the Sanctuary."

"Hi, Deirdre. how do I reach you?" the girl asked curiously.

"Oh, just speak my name and what you need. We have a system, sort of an intercom."

Linn remembered her manners. "Thank you. It looks delicious."

"You're welcome. I have to run...." Deirdre bounced away.

Linn applied herself to her breakfast and Hypatia sipped her juice in silence for a while. Gareth and Blackie both strolled in, looking smug. She guessed they had been well-fed when they declined a taste of her ham. They sat with her for a minute, and then slipped away again.

Finished, Linn gathered her dishes and Hypatia showed her the pass through, where she handed them to another smiling coblyn.

"How many of them are there?" she asked the scholar.

"Oh, hundreds at least. It's like a small coblyn town here in the Sanctuary. In exchange for their living, they work various jobs to keep it running smoothly." Hypatia led her into another tunnel.

"I'm having trouble telling some of them apart." Linn admitted ruefully, following her.

"Oh, I'm fairly sure they do that on purpose."

Linn laughed. "Well, ok, I guess that just keeps guests guessing, then. I mean, I'd know Deirdre or Daffyd on sight, but most of them don't introduce themselves."

"Names are important to the coblyns. They rarely gift them to others, and never to a stranger."

Hypatia led Linn out into an unfamiliar tunnel, and then briskly down it to a door with the word "Scholar" engraved on it. Hypatia touched the carving. "Flattering, this, it was in place and ready for me when I arrived. I didn't even know I was coming, but your grandparents prepared."

Linn chuckled. "That's Grampa Heff, the oldest boy scout."

"Hmmm.... I wonder how well he knew Baden-Powell." Linn boggled at that thought and Hypatia smiled, and pushed the door open. "Welcome to the Scholar's lair, dear."

Linn stepped in gingerly. There was paper everywhere. Books, towers of them, regular printer paper, what looked an awful lot like ancient papyrus scrolls. Hypatia bustled through it and lifted a stack off a wing chair.

"Here you are... Let me see." She turned to the large desk, obscured with teetering stacks of books and paper. Lifting a pile and setting it on top of another, which made Linn want to jump forward to prevent certain collapse, she exclaimed, "Aha, here it is."

Miraculously, the tower of papers she had just made stayed still while Hypatia lifted out a sleek laptop and handed it to Linn. "This is for you, Linn."

"Mine?"

"Yes, your grandmother said you should have a good one."

Linn blinked, looking down at the pretty machine. "Cool..."

Hypatia sat down behind the desk, opening drawers. "And here are the cords. I hope you know how to use them, I certainly don't."

Linn took the bag of cords and looked in it. "I think I can figure it out. I'm not a geek, really, but I usually make it work."

"Good, good. I'm afraid I'm rather old-school. The internet just annoys me, but I'm told it's a good research tool."

"It can be... but there's a lot of junk on it, too."

"You are now in charge of it." Hypatia assured her solemnly.

Linn laughed at the idea of being in charge of the world wide web. "All right."

"Before we start, I know you want to understand what we are doing here."

"As much as I'm allowed, yes." Linn looked for an outlet and plugged the power cord in. The laptop had no charge on it.

Hypatia got up and closed the door.

"According to me, you are allowed to know all of it. But you will have to figure some of it out on your own."

25

PLAN OF ATTACK

*L*inn felt rather like a junior spy about to get her first briefing. She steadied the closed laptop on her knees and prepared to listen.

"What do you know about immortals, my dear?"

"Um..." Linn was taken off guard. She had not expected a question. "I know they aren't from Earth, originally. I don't think they have a form, per se. I'm trying to figure out if they are maybe..." she waved her hands in the air, searching for the right words. "Maybe pure energy, or nannite people, or something. Coyote gave me some books and that was a theme in all of them. I think it was a clue. You aren't magical, just something really... alien. And I think maybe immortals brought humans to life. Or something like that."

She paused, thinking. Hypatia clapped, startling her.

"Oh, bravo, Linnaea! You are quite clever!"

The old woman beamed at her, and Linn felt her cheeks warm.

"I've been given a lot of hints." The girl demurred.

"You've listened to them, and strung them together. Not many could do that."

"I know you aren't omniscient, or omnipotent." Linn kept thinking out loud, now.

"No, we neither see and know everything, nor are we all-powerful. Which is a good thing." Hypatia's voice was dry at that last.

"Yes, I'm learning that." Linn sighed. "Tia, I know Grampa said immortals can't die, but why aren't there more of them?"

"Ah. The question that lies at the core of our research. Immortals might not die... but they may not choose to live, or remain sane, either. That many years... all those memories..." Her eyes clouded and she looked off into the distance for a long time, silent.

"I know," Linn began quietly after a time. "That the forms they use can die. The girls went through that. I think... that the forms you use age. Or you choose to age. I'm honestly not sure which."

"Death and aging, the most wanted answers humanity has today." Tia looked at Linn. "You understand why you could not be told before."

"Yes, I think so. If there had been a way..." her voice faltered, and she thought of Cora, the night before, giving her father's love to her. "To keep my father with me."

"Your mother would have done it. She is not an Old One, she gave no vows. In some ways, she is one of the sparks that lit the fire we must now walk through."

"I thought so." Linn sighed. "So, it's not that easy."

"No, it isn't. Immortals can't cease to exist. We can, however, choose to sleep. We can be imprisoned. We can, in a sense, imprison ourselves."

"Is that what happened with Loki?"

Hypatia looked startled. "How did you know about that?"

"Coyote and Bes both talk about him like he's their friend, but only ever in the past tense, like he's dead. Only he can't be."

The Scholar sighed. "The entire Norse family is... asleep."

"Fimbulwinter?"

"You are a child after my own heart." Hypatia clucked her approval at Linn's deductions. "Most of the Old Ones lacked a certain mental flexibility. Loki could have survived, but his heart wasn't in it. He chose to follow them into the winter." Hypatia looked sad.

"I don't think that helps us, though." Linn said thoughtfully. They couldn't discourage all the mad gods into giving up.

"No, I think you are right. We need an actual weapon."

"A weapon could hurt us... well, Mom and my grandparents, and you... as well." Linn sighed.

Hypatia smiled at her sadly. "Yes, it could. You carry a sword."

Linn put her hand on Lambent's pommel. She had gotten so used to carrying it over the last couple of months, she didn't even think about buckling her on in the morning. She supposed it made her feel closer to Grampa Heff.

"Yes."

"And she has two edges. One cuts toward you, the other away from you."

Linn nodded. She could see what Tia was saying.

"So, what are we doing?" She let go of Lambent and pressed the power button on the laptop.

"We are trying to find a way to kill immortals." Hypatia informed her calmly, her scarred old face not even changing expression.

Linn felt the words hit her with a physical force behind them. She looked down at the smooth surface of the laptop she was holding, seeing a dim reflection of herself in it. She was so serious...

They didn't talk for a while. Hypatia picked up a scroll, letting Linn think. Linn was grateful. She wasn't sure she wanted to find a way to kill anyone. Much less something that could take the people she loved most from her. Finally, she looked up.

"I don't know why we need to do this."

Hypatia put the scroll down and smiled sadly.

"There are hundreds of immortals living amongst humans. Thousands more sleep... death in a dream state. Any one of us has the power to destroy humanity."

"But... how?"

"You don't ask why."

"I think I've figure out why. Most of the Old Ones think of humans as cattle, or at best, pets. Now there are too many of us, and we are gaining a knowledge of technology that could actually harm them."

Hypatia nodded. "The how is a little more complicated. Simplest, of course, would be to unleash a plague. The Black Death, the Spanish flu...

many others. They were tools of certain immortals for their own ends and means."

"You can manipulate yourself on a genetic level." Linn mused, thinking that was how Bes had kept looking younger and younger during their time together.

"Smaller even than that. You know we use something we call the High Path?"

"Yes, it's a way to travel. I can't do it, so it must be something only an immortal can do."

"Well, you might be able to when you come into your full power and learn to use it. But have you ever heard of Quantum Tunneling?"

"Um... maybe in a science fiction story?" Linn wrinkled her nose, thinking.

"Ah, then, your first assignment. Look it up, dear." Hypatia picked up the scroll again and Linn knew she wasn't going to get any more from her for a while.

Looking down at her laptop, she opened a new browser window.

2 6

SEARCH AND PERHAPS RESCUE

Sekhmet sighed. There were times she was really glad humans were so easy to make look-don't-see. This was one of them. The Atlantic Ocean was a huge body of water. You could travel over it for days and never see anyone, most of the time. Today was not one of them. The area they were in was swarming with rescue craft. There wasn't anything to rescue.

The plane had hit the water hard, and almost five hundred people had perished instantly. Pieces of wreckage was scattered for literally miles now, some floating, others somewhere below them. She, Steve, and Pele were sitting cross-legged just over the surface of the water. A bubble of power surrounded them, keeping them warm and dry. They were waiting.

Helicopters buzzed overhead. Steve looked up. "Those look like fun, you know?"

"You're such a little boy at heart." Sekhmet chuckled.

"Yeah, it's what you love about me." He flashed back.

Pele laughed. "The child in all of us keeps us sane. I hate to remind you of why we are here... But the Naiads are coming now."

Sekhmet looked down between her paws. The tawny pads hovered about a foot above the waves. The water was opaque today, dark and sullen.

"It's a good thing we aren't human." The big cat said quietly.

"So much death, and yet we walk unscathed through all of it." Pele commented softly in agreement with the unspoken thoughts.

"Here they are." Steve was looking down to one side.

Sekhmet saw a flicker of white as the water dwelling immortals came close to the surface. She could see their faces, then they emerged directly below the immortals, lifting a glowing orb toward them. High, whispering voices spoke in unison.

"We have found them. Take them, please, before we all cry..."

Sekhmet could see that the four Naiads all had tears streaming from their eyes. They referred to the untold numbers of other Naiads who lived in the Atlantic Ocean. Each body of water was occupied with a family who were all connected closely.

Pele reached down and took the artifact. Tears pooled in her eyes.

"What is it?" Sekhmet could tell the crying was uncontrollable.

"So much pain... The children. The laume, their mother, is wrapped around them. They are so afraid..." Her voice dropped to a whisper.

"What do we do?" Steve asked in concern.

"Let's take them to land, first." Pele sounded choked up.

Steve and Sekhmet each took her elbows and carried her, as both her hands were clasped on the globe, which was the concentrated essences of three immortals, so tightly wrapped together they were actually palpable at the moment.

Sekhmet could sense Pele probing with her power at the laume while they ran the high path. She couldn't feel anything from the globe except pain. Her heart thudded in her chest as they ran, and she could feel herself beginning to cry silent tears.

She stumbled when they touched ground and fell to her knees. Steve let go of Pele and doubled over, sucking deep, sobbing breaths in as though he hadn't been able to breathe for a long time. Pele, tears streaming down her face, continued to walk ahead blindly once they let go of her. Sekhmet changed to cat form and caught up with her, looking around to see where they were. Pele had guided their travels.

"Where are we?" Steve, back in jaguar form as well, asked her, swinging his heavy black head from side to side. The terrain was bleak. And cold... Sekhmet shivered, not just from the temperature.

"Iceland, I think." She told him after a moment.

Pele kept walking without looking and the two cats flanked her, constantly scanning for movement. Nothing should be here, and yet Sekhmet knew Steve felt the same way she did. Jumpy, off balance...

Pele wasn't talking, and Sekhmet was beginning to get worried. Whatever the laume was doing, she might be drawing the Hawaiian goddess into it. The children's mother was a Lithuanian fairy, a family of immortals Sekhmet was not familiar with. Something was wrong here. Sekhmet had seen immortals withdraw before, shrinking away from pain, but never like this.

"Pele. Pele!" She shouted at the woman.

Pele stopped, and then slowly looked at Sekhmet. "I need to put them someplace warm."

Sekhemet looked in the direction they were going. "You want to throw them in there?" She asked in disbelief. The volcano goddess had been rumored to require certain sacrifices in the past.

"No, no. Just... close." Pele reassured her.

Sekhmet looked back at the volcano. "I'm not sure about this."

"She wants... warmth. And to be alone. She doesn't want anyone near her or her children." Pele didn't explain how she knew this.

The big cat sighed. "All right. Keep going. Let's get this done, it can't be good for you, either."

They walked on, sometimes stumbling over the rough terrain, until they came to a fumarole, gently steaming from the ground. Pele knelt and scooped a shallow hole in the loose ashy soil. Steve and Sekhmet helped her dig, as their paws were better prepared for it than her human hands were. Pele laid the globe into it and let go. Murmuring something in Hawaiian, she stood and they buried the globe.

Pele gasped when it disappeared from sight and staggered a little. She put a hand to her heart and drew a deep breath.

"That was... bad." she told her concerned companions. Sekhmet thought that was an understatement from her friend's pallor.

"Let's go." Sekhmet said. She wanted to get as far away from here as she could. "Pele. can you get back to the Sanctuary by yourself? I think we need to tell Heff about this."

The older woman nodded. She looked tired. "I need to get to the other children."

Sekhmet know what she meant. She could do with a peaceful moment of cuddling, right now, of knowing all was well.

"Go. I will be there when I can. Give them my love." She licked Pele's cheek.

"Mine, too." Steve's quiet bass rumble was solemn for once.

Pele bent and hugged him. He arched his head into her and purred. "I will be careful." He said.

Pele hugged Sekhmet next. "I will be careful, also." The big cat told the old goddess. "This was a fluke. It's not an attack that will work on us."

"I know. But still..."

Sekhmet knew what she meant. This attack, on a weak immortal and her children, was something that was rarely done. And the tragic result... the living death of three beings, would have dire consequences.

"We leave a marker. There will be a time we can return for them. But now, we run." She said finally. She and Steve leapt up, into the high path, simultaneously.

Pele was left standing in the lonely wind for a long time before she finally gathered her fleeting thoughts and leapt upward onto the Path.

27

RESEARCHERS

*L*inn looked up from her reading and rubbed her eyes. Then she looked back down at the computer clock.

"Darn." She muttered. Then, feeling slightly foolish, she said out loud. "Deirdre? Lunch for two in the Scholar's office?"

Hypatia didn't even look up from the book she was handling with cotton gloves on. "Just a salad for me."

"A sandwich, I guess. I don't care what." Linn added, then stood up and put the laptop in her chair. "Tia?"

"Yes, Child?" the old woman still didn't look up.

"I'm going to stretch my legs. It's after lunch time."

"Go ahead. I'm used to this." Hypatia looked up finally and smiled briefly. "You are used to a much more active life, I'm sure."

Linn felt a little sheepish. "Yes, I am. I'll be back in a few."

The tunnel here was painted a warm cream, but with nothing on the walls it was very empty and she heard echoes as her footsteps made sound. She walked toward the Library. She hadn't been in it yet, but she knew it was down this way. As she walked, she pulled her phone and earbuds out of her pocket.

Linn had tried to call her mother when she first arrived, and had gotten her voicemail. She wasn't worried about her. If something were wrong Hypatia would have let her know. Pele was on her way back, she guessed. Linn would ask her when she was home. She put the earbuds in and started to dance along to one of her favorite songs, letting the movement take the stiffness out of her muscles.

After two songs she stopped and took the earbuds out. She felt better... energized. And starving. She headed back to the office. The doors further down the tunnel swung open and her grandmother stepped through.

"Grandma!"

She ran forward to hug Pele, who held her close for a long time without speaking. Linn waited, dying to know what was going on, but hesitant to speak until she knew her grandmother was ready to talk.

"Linn, I am so glad you are here."

"I'm happy to be here, too. The kittens are safe, Hypatia is awesome, and the coblyns are pretty nifty, too. What's wrong?" Linn let it all out in one breathless rush.

Pele sighed into Linn's hair, not letting go. "You remember the twins that were flying in from Lithuania?"

"Yeah?" Linn frowned, tipping her head back to see her grandmother's face. Pele looked unbearably sad.

"The Old Ones brought down the plane."

"Brought it down?" Linn felt bewildered.

"It crashed in the ocean. Everyone onboard was killed."

"How many?" Linn whispered, holding onto her grandmother tighter. She couldn't see her eyes, just the flickers of power.

"Almost five hundred people."

"All to harm those children. What happened to them?"

"Oh, ku'o aloha..."

Linn felt her eyes well up. "How did they take the plane down?" she demanded raggedly.

Pele shrugged helplessly. "An Old One in insubstantial form could have taken the electrical system down..."

Linn felt like a million light bulbs had just gone off in her head. She pulled away from her grandmother's arms. "I have to ask Hypatia something."

She marched back into the office, wiping her eyes roughly. "Tia, are immortals affected by electricity... would an EMP take you out?"

Hypatia looked up at her in confusion. "I don't know."

Pele following Linn into the office, lifted her hand to the Scholar, who took it in her own. They stood in silence for a moment. Linn picked up the laptop and sat down, typing quickly.

"Look. There was a test called Starfish a long time ago near Hawaii, it says it affected the electricity here. Grandma, did you feel it?"

Pele nodded. "I was very weak for a long time after that. Your grandfather helped me through that time, which led to your mother." She smiled at Linn. That had obviously been a happy thought, but Linn really didn't want to know more.

Linn looked at Hypatia. "Electro-magnetic Pulse. It shuts down electrical systems. If immortals are really energy beings who exist by the electromagnetic charge between electrons and can form their own atoms..."

Pele and Hypatia looked at each other.

"She's brilliant, you know." Hypatia told Linn's grandmother.

"I know." Her grandmother grinned, breaking through her sorrow for the first time.

They both smiled at Linn, who was hovering between embarrassment and a shivery feeling that these women could be scary if they chose. The expressions they were wearing were fierce.

"If we could detonate something like Starfish near them..." she suggested. "We could sting them and persuade them to stop."

Hypatia rubbed her eyes. "Linn, Deirdre left your sandwich here. I hate to do this, but could you take it to the common room?"

Linn nodded. She understood they needed to talk to Grampa Heff. She wasn't old enough to be a part of what was coming next. She took the plate and walked out of the room, swallowing the lump in her throat. She had just come up with something that could hurt someone she knew... someone she loved.

In the common room she found a quiet corner and watched kids playing while she picked at her sandwich. Blackie appeared silently at her elbow and she offered him some of the tuna from her meal. He ate it politely, and then flowed into her lap. She could swear he had grown already; he was hanging off on both sides. She stroked his head and he started to purr.

She sighed and let the tension flow out of her. "Kitten therapy. Thanks, Blackie. You are a sweetheart."

Juggling him and the plate, she stood. He had definitely grown, and she couldn't carry him far. "You want to walk, or what?" Linn asked him. He looked at her and flowed down onto the floor. "Thanks, kitten. Come on."

She turned in her plate at the pass through and decided she wanted to be outside. Returning to her room, she put on her suit, which had been cleaned, and went down to the beach.

It wasn't deserted out there, but the girls just waved and went back to playing with the kitsune. They had an elaborate sand castle going on. Linn walked down to the far corner of the beach, trying not to think, letting her hair blow in the wind. By the time she had gotten down there she had decided it was impossible to stop thinking entirely.

She stood looking out at the Pacific. The blueness of it reminded her that she had seen Blackie's power. She looked back up the beach. He had joined the others in playing. Right at the moment he seemed to be digging a hole. She focused on them. Power shimmered like a haze over the whole beach, an aurora of colors. Much of it was her grandmother's, she saw. Which made sense.

"Power." Linn whispered. "What is it? A nannite cloud? So, what keeps it in check? Why are the children of a human and an immortal even viable, much less only half-strength?"

She realized she might never know the answers unless one of them decided to tell her. One of the oldest, since she suspected the younger generations hadn't been told everything, either. Walking back toward the Sanctuary, she knew what she was going to be when she grew up.

"I don't think they even know. Not really." She said aloud, feeling the wind take the words from her lips as she spoke.

She didn't say anything else until she was back in her room. She went in the bathroom and looked in the mirror. She was still the same as she had been that morning. "I ought to look different." Linn told her reflection. 'It would be more satisfying if I looked different. Older, or something."

The reflection remained unchanged. Linn was glad, actually. It would have freaked her out to have it start answering back. She walked into the other room and threw herself down on the bed, closing her eyes.

She fell asleep after about the three hundred and fortieth sheep. And woke up falling again, sitting bolt upright on the bed. Someone had been calling her, she was sure. She sat in the now dark room and listened hard. Silence. She rubbed her face. It must have been in her dream she'd heard her name.

She went out into the other room. Everything was dark and quiet. She looked at her watch, with the tritium hands she could see in the dark. It was after midnight. Linn sighed. She didn't want to disturb anyone. She started to go back into her room when Daffyd walked out of the tunnel carrying a small lamp.

"Ah, you're awake. Good..."

"Hello. Um... You were looking for me?" She looked at him in confusion, not sure he had the right person.

"Yes, your grandfather wants to talk to you. You should probably dress."

"Oh," Linn looked down. She had pulled a robe on. "Just a minute."

She threw on shorts and a tee shirt, and then, automatically, Lambent. Which felt odd with the shorts, but she didn't feel like jeans, it was warm in the Sanctuary.

Daffyd was waiting for her with what she tentatively thought was a mining lamp. He led the way through the rooms and tunnels to a door she hadn't been seen before. It swung open at his touch.

"Here she is," he said, stepping aside for Linn to enter.

Linn walked through the doorway and stopped. She felt very young and grubby suddenly. She'd thought she was going to meet her grandfather... there were a lot of people here, all in odd garbs and all looking grim.

"Linnaea." Heff stepped away from the long table to take her hand. She let him lead her forward. He turned to the assembled council and said simply. "My granddaughter."

Linn looked around and saw her grandmother, Hypatia... there was Quetzalcoatl, resplendent in an iridescent white suit. She blinked at that; it was rather loud.

"Why is she here?" A tall immortal she didn't recognize demanded. He was dressed in lion skins that contrasted with his deep black skin. She looked at his and focused. His power was a light golden yellow in color.

"She will lead a team of coblyns to the launch site, where they will make any needed repairs, and then the warhead will be launched."

"But why send a child?" He leaned forward, and Linn was surprised to realize he was concerned for her, not angry at her presence as she initially assumed.

"Because I need someone who isn't a beacon of power. I don't have any other halflings on hand, and I know she can do this. Daffyd..." Heff turned to the diminutive immortal. "Will you follow her?"

"Yes, we will." The goblin king assured him gravely.

Heff turned back. Linn was getting the feeling this was not new ground. "They will leave tomorrow afternoon before dusk, which gives the rest of us time to get in place."

Much later, Linn stood beside the zodiac remembering the rest of his briefing, most of it intended for her. The coblyns were terrible at getting around aboveground. Her orienteering training was going to come in handy. Once she'd been dismissed, with a brief hug from her grandfather, she had given up on sleep, instead going to the Scholar's office.

Somewhere a topo map had been found and she had it, ready for the mission, but she wanted to see what they were getting into. It took her just minutes to find the location, and she zoomed in on the location, staring at the bunkers. Four rectangular depressions in the green on one side, each with a white courtyard? She wasn't sure what it was, but it was some kind of concrete pad. Those were the munitions bunkers. The two dark green slits in the ground were ditches for the launchers, she had been told.

Blackie bumped her hand and brought Linn back to the present. "Hey, you aren't supposed to be here." She told him. He just looked at her steadily, his eyes glowing. She sighed.

"Daffyd?" She looked around for the goblin king.

"Yes, child?" He appeared at her elbow, making her jump.

Linn thought if the fiction was that she was supposed to be leading them was to hold up, he shouldn't call her child.

"Blackie wants to go."

"Well, at least we don't need to camouflage him." Was the cheerful response.

Linn snorted. They had painted her face green and brown. With their green skin they blended with the lush vegetation well. She looked down at the kitten. "Don't you dare put your claws out in that rubber boat," she threatened him.

He flattened his ears at her. She put a hand on his head, realizing as she did so that he really had grown... or chosen to get bigger... as he was waist high to her now. As high as he was in the dream.

"Time to go, Linn." Daffyd interrupted her train of thought softly. She climbed into the zodiac awkwardly. She'd never been in one before. Blackie flowed in softly, his pads careful on the bottom. He had taken her seriously. They were pulled off the beach by Naiads, who would take them to their destination beach.

Linn sat on the surface of the water, feeling it under her butt, only a layer of rubber between her and the ocean. She shivered. Daffyd gripped her shoulder.

"The Naiads are bringing a fog to cover us."

She just nodded. She'd known that was coming. She went over the map again in her head. The ocean was abnormally calm, little waves slapping at the boats.

They were headed for Dillingham Airfield, and having looked at the maps she had decided they would land at Mokuleia Beach Park. It was going to be a long day. Daffyd had started the quiet little motor and was leaning on it contemplatively, not looking like he was going to talk much. Blackie was asleep, or faking it well. Linn just felt like she was going to throw up.

Supposedly none of the enemy had any idea what they were up to. This was supposed to be a walk in the park. Or at least a walk in the dark, wet woods. The munitions bunkers hadn't been used in three decades. They looked from the satellite shots like they were pretty overgrown.

When Linn could finally hear the roar of the surf she sighed with relief. This might be the most dangerous part of the mission, but at least she had a job to do. The sitting and waiting was going to kill her.

"Ready?" Daffyd asked Loudly enough for her to hear over the surf. There was no point in trying to be quiet, the waves would cover any sound. The tricky part was going over unfamiliar ground in the dark, while trying not to be seen. The coblyns were under orders not to use excess power that might attract the wrong kind of attention.

"Ready," Linn replied, picking up her pack. She would put it on once on land. If she fell overboard with it on it would drag her down.

She crouched and held onto the straps as the Naiads surfed the little boat through the waves. The grate of sand under her feet almost knocked her on her face. She was out of the boat on that momentum, Blackie just ahead of her and Daffyd behind her. A swarm of silent coblyns accompanied them, her team of twelve engineers for the Nike.

The thick fog obscured much of the beach, but the pure white sand made it easier to see as they trotted across it. With the cool, damp fog, there were no humans on the beach, Linn was relieved to note. The hardest part came next.

On the verge of Highway 930, they stopped and listened. No car engines broke the eerie quiet of the fog. Linn had them cross in groups of three. She was the last one to go. All was still. When she reached the other side, she could see the coblyns doing something to the fence.

"Linn, close your eyes and let me lead you." Daffyd asked.

"I thought I was leading." the nervous girl snapped. This was going too easily. The fog was worrying her, and she kept thinking of her dream.

"You are. It's just this... is dangerous. There is no try, only do or not do."

Linn was startled into a laugh, which she quickly suppressed. "You did that on purpose."

"Of course. I'm well aware of the resemblance. Only I'm older than nine hundred years."

She sighed. "All right, Daffy, I trust you." Closing her eyes and holding out her hands, she whispered, "That sounds so wrong..."

There was a brief tingle, and then Daffyd told her she could open her eyes again. She looked around her. They were on the other side of the fence, but it looked intact.

"I'll think about that one later." she promised herself. Daffy just chuckled.

Dillingham airport was no longer very active, and with the fog any air travel was socked in. Still, she wanted to get across the airstrip as fast as possible. This time, they all ran as a group. She could barely see the huge number twenty-six that was one of her landmarks on the place to cross the airstrip.

Once they were across, they stopped briefly to regroup and let Linn orient herself with the map and compass. She pointed in the direction they needed to go and they set off through the fog. She was looking for the long-unused taxiway that jutted off the landward side of the airstrip. They found it in about five minutes, and she led them up it.

She relaxed a little as they hiked along the crumbling asphalt. Being out on the airstrip made her feel exposed. Now it was a matter of not getting lost in the heavy fog. She knew from the mental picture in her head that there was open cropland off to their left side, and a double row of planted trees to the right. What she could see was gray, and the ground in front of her, ancient asphalt with weeds coming up through it.

She stopped and listened. Nothing. It was like being wrapped in a wet wool blanket. Daffyd touched her shoulder. She checked the compass and they veered to the right slightly.

"I wish the fog would lift a little."

Daffyd chuckled. "Oh, it's a good thing. trust me, I've done a few of these outings."

"Then why am I along?"

"Our sense of direction is terrible." he admitted cheerfully. "We always need a human or guide to find our objective above ground. We're engineers, not orienteers. Keep going, girl."

"So, what happens when we get there?"

"We assess the Nike your grandfather hid, repair if needed, load the warhead onto it, and launch it. From there..." he shrugged. "Not my worry."

"The coblyns don't worry much, do they?" she voiced a thought she'd had for a while now.

"It's not natural to us, no." He admitted that cheerfully. She supposed it was a perk, now that she'd learned that she couldn't stop thinking.

She stumbled at the edge of a wash out. "Here it is..." she said. "Now, right off here..."

The path was right where it was supposed to be. Hung over with wet vegetation from the fog, she was soaked by the time they had taken a dozen steps into the woods. She shivered at the touch of a vine down the back of her neck. It wasn't cold, just really wet. She was starting to feel claustrophobic in the fog.

She knew from the satellite photos that the path wound down through the bunkers. It led to a big, grassy area behind them, and Heff had said it was probably made by cattle. If they stayed on the path they couldn't get lost now.

Linn felt tense. Nothing was happening. It seemed to her that something ought to happen. They were on a clandestine expedition, and there should be trouble, right? She rolled her shoulders, feeling the weight of the pack.

The bunkers were much larger in person than they looked on the satellite photos. She stopped dead as they entered the clearing. She knew it was the clearing because the fog was marginally lighter. A cow stood in front of her, looking at her curiously. Several others loomed in the fog.

"We're here." She told Daffyd. Blackie scooted his head under her hand. His fur was soaking wet. "How long is this going to take? It's getting dark and we are all wet. I want to build a fire and get dry."

"Good idea. I don't know how long it will take. It all depends how well the government sealed the bunkers before they abandoned this site."

"Oh, well, then we will be here awhile."

Daffyd laughed at her sarcasm. "We will open a bunker and you can get out of the wet."

Linn nodded and let the team go to work. The four coblyns who had been carrying the warhead came and set it down next to her. She eyed the metal cylinder dubiously.

"It isn't radioactive," one of them assured her.

"Great." She replied shortly, feeling grumpy. The fog and the fear were getting to her. And this thing was not her idea of company.

2 8

CLARKE'S LAW

*L*inn was watching the coblyns at the bunker access door. They were holding their hands over it and chanting something softly. The Coblyn standing with her followed her gaze.

"It looks like magic." Linn muttered.

"Do you know Clarke's third law?" The unnamed one asked quietly.

"The one about technology?"

"'Any sufficiently advanced technology is indistinguishable from magic.' That's the one."

Linn looked down at him. "I thought you weren't supposed to tell me these kinds of things."

"Nothing you didn't already know. You might not be able to put a name to it just yet, is all." He didn't look up at her, just spoke casually, but she felt like she'd been granted a glimpse of a secret.

She stood thinking for a long moment, then asked, "I know you don't like to give out your names, do you mind if I call you Clark?"

He looked up at her and grinned. It was a slightly horrifying sight with his wrinkly green skin and snaggly teeth, but she was used to coblyns now.

"I'd be honored." He assured her with a chuckle.

She smiled back. "So, they are affecting the molecular structure of the door. Why the chanting?"

"Tradition!" He laughed. "Come on, they've got it open."

Linn led the way to the now open door. When she stepped through it, a wave of musty odor rolled over her.

"Gah!" she sneezed. Moldy dankness assaulted her senses. It was pitch dark in there, too. She fumbled a headlight out of her pocket and switched it on. The beam of light showed her an empty hallway.

Blackie stayed on her flank as she walked forward into the hallway. At the end of the hallway there was an ordinary door. Linn tried the handle and was surprised when it turned and the door swung open.

She stepped into a big, open room. Her headlight didn't reach very far. She picked out shrouded shapes but that was all. Blackie prowled past her, and into the darkness. She wasn't worried, his eyes were better in the dark than hers.

She stepped back into the hall when Daffyd called her name.

"I'm here."

"I think you'll be more comfortable in an office. I think building a fire in the missile room would be a bad idea."

She could not see him, but could imagine the grin that went with that little speech.

"Sounds better to me, too." she admitted.

She retraced her steps up the hall. She half expected to see her own footprints in the dust, but there was no dust in the hall. Daffyd held a door open for her.

"You can see in the dark?"

"Of course. Welsh mining, remember?"

"Someday I want a story from you." she told him as she stepped into the bare office. The floor was tiled. "I don't think I can build a fire in here."

"No need."

He knelt on the floor and put his hands together. Murmuring so softly Linn couldn't catch what he was saying, he slowly spread them apart and a small fire appeared, the flames flickering cheerfully in yellow and green. He stepped back and bowed a little. "We will be in the missile room if you need anything."

Linn was left alone in the room with the fire, which gave off a warm glow, but, and she inspected it as closely as she dared, floated about an inch off the floor.

"That's it. I'm calling it magic."

She took her pack off and sat next to the little fire, peeling off her already steaming layers down to her undershirt. There was nothing to hang them on, so she arranged them near the fire. She was reluctant to venture back outside. The coblyns had work to do, which did not include bodyguarding a teenager. She'd sit tight until they were ready to go again.

Linn skinned down to her underwear, leaving her jeans there to dry with her boots. She got up and walked around the room. It was square, and empty. Stains on the walls from moisture gave her the idea there had been shelves and cabinets, but they were long gone.

She pulled an energy bar out of her pack and nibbled on it. She was tired, and feeling rather let down. All that secrecy and everything had gone off without a hitch. She leaned on her pack and let the fire warm her, her eyes drifting closed.

She woke up with a jolt. She'd slid onto the floor, her head pillowed on her arm. Blackie was curled up along her side. She was stiff and sore. Her mouth felt like cotton. She lay still for a second, wondering what had woken her up. She could hear a faint murmur of voices through the open door.

Linn staggered to her feet. She didn't feel rested. Everything that had happened over the last few days was weighing on her. She picked up her clothes and redressed. They were dry, the little green fire still glowing cheerfully. She squinted at it. There was a little pink in the flames, now. Had she done that?

Not bothering with her boots, she padded down the hall, carrying Lambent's sheath in one hand. She poked her head into the missile room. The coblyns had lit more of their fires here, and the room was bathed in a strange green light. They all stood around an empty spot on the floor in a rough oval shape.

Linn backed out of the doorway silently, not wanting to disturb them. She walked back to her little room. She rubbed her temple with her free hand. She wasn't sure what they were doing, and she wasn't sure how this weapon was going to be deployed. She knew she couldn't be told everything, but it was still driving her nuts.

Blackie was still asleep. She sat cross-legged next to him and drank water, hoping it would clear her head. People were dead. The children who were traveling to Sanctuary had been lost to pain and terror. The entire human race was in danger. It was all coming down to twelve little green guys, her, and an oversized kitten.

Not that she was doing anything. Sitting in a moldy room waiting wasn't helping. She stood up and belted on Lambent, then pulled on her boots. She'd go check and make sure everything was alright outside. If all twelve of the coblyns were working inside, no one was standing sentry. She knew how to charge a ward, maybe she could set one.

She slipped outside into the fog. She wondered how long she'd been asleep and checked her watch. It had been six hours since they had arrived here. Shouldn't the fog have lifted? She looked around. If anything, it was heavier than it had been when they got here. Blackie joined her, bumping her hand with his cold, wet nose.

"Hey." She rubbed his ears. "It's spooky out here, don't you think?"

He looked up at her and nodded. Linn felt her jaw drop. "You're talking to me now?" There was a squeak in her voice.

He smiled at her, his fangs showing. Linn leaned down and hugged him. "Ok, you're so darn cute. Want to help me make sure no one is sneaking up on us?"

He nodded again, then walked off into the fog. Linn followed him just before his long black tail disappeared. She quickly realized that if anyone was out there, she wasn't going to see them. She almost bumped into a tree.

"Ok, I'm going to try this." she told Blackie.

She put her hands on the wet bark, feeling the roughness scratch her palms a little. She focused on the tree, startled to see it had a faint energy of its own. She couldn't even read a color it was so minute. She thought about setting a ward, concentrating hard. A spark of pink jumped into the tree and she jerked back at the sting. A tiny thread of power stretched from her to the tree.

Linn walked to the corner of the bunker. She knew she couldn't set them all the way around it; she didn't have much to give and it was just too big. She put her hands on the crumbling concrete and repeated the process. Afterward, she rubbed her hands to try and make the feeling come back. Blackie licked her fingers.

"Ouch." she told him. "No, not you. Every time I use power it stings."

He looked up at her, his fuzzy eyebrows bunched together. She read concern in his face.

"It's ok. If anyone comes near the bunker I'll know once I set one more. Then I'll stop."

She walked to the far end of the bunker, picking her way around the rampant vegetation. She leaned on the concrete and took a deep breath. Blackie reared up and put his paws on her hands. She focused, and saw a spark of pink, but it didn't hurt.

"I don't know how you did that..." she told the cat. "But thank you."

He hopped down and went off into the fog. She sighed. Back to the empty room for however long it was going to take. She looked up at the gray sky, thinking she might see the sun burn through. It certainly was lighter out. She knew she'd feel better when the fog was gone.

They couldn't leave until nightfall, anyway. She wondered where Grampa was, and Bes, and Sekhmet. She knew they couldn't die... but she also knew now they could be terribly hurt. She walked back inside the bunker.

The coblyns were now standing around a visible missile and a clean patch on the floor. The open space must have been... They had broken through whatever her grandfather had done to hide it from the military when they abandoned this facility. They were still chanting, though, and she wondered what exactly they were doing. Repairing it at the atomic level? Her stomach rumbled.

Backing away from the door to not startle them, she thought about food, patting her stomach. She had enough materials on hand for a couple of spartan meals, and the coblyns were going to need a break soon, she was sure.

It made her feel better to do something. She cut sticks and rigged a tripod for her little cooking pot. Soup would be warm and good in the damp bunker. Water, vegetable chips... she wished she could gather some fruit from the woods that surrounded the bunker, she knew she'd find guava and mangoes easily. Wandering in the woods was right out, though.

Bouillon cubes and dried noodles that she set aside to wait for a boil. They might have to eat out of the same pot. She didn't have bowls. Hopefully the coblyns had spoons, she didn't have those, either. She picked up a scrap of wood, sniffed it for bitterness. It didn't smell bad. Linn started to whittle a spoon with her belt knife, which with the five-inch blade was tricky.

Blackie padded in and dropped two chickens at her feet. Linn laughed. "Wow! Thank you, big guy. Are these your first kill?"

He stood there smiling at her. She ruffled his ears and praised him lavishly. "These will make lunch much nicer. You're amazing!"

He plopped down near the fire and started to wash his paws. Linn took the birds outside to clean them. After skinning them and burying the waste deep enough to keep it from scavengers, she carefully washed her hands in a pool of water that had collected in the corner of the courtyard. She'd use alcohol to kill germs, but the yuck she wanted off her skin.

Back inside, she boned the birds. They were skinny little things. Hawaii was plagued with feral chickens, and Blackie had just helped reduce that population. Even without much meat on their bones they would add lots of flavor to the soup.

She didn't hear Daffyd until he started to laugh. She looked over her shoulder at the coblyns, who were standing in the doorway. She smiled and waved at the pot, "Lunch!"

She was sitting cross-legged by the fire, stirring the noodles. She held up the makeshift spoon. "I hope you guys brought your own spoons. I have two, now."

Now all the little men burst into laughter.

29

THE HIGH BATTLE

Sekhmet stood on the endless plain in human form, the wind whipping her skirts around her legs. She brushed the hair out of her eyes, adjusted her bow and quiver, then turned to Steve and hissed, "Tell me again why we are fighting like this?"

He looked morose. "Don't ask me. I'd give my left dew claw for a AK 47 about now."

They stared across the field at the line of the other army, all dressed as they were in ancient garb and carrying period weapons. In the center of the field, the generals had met for a parlay.

"They can't let go of the past." Sekhmet said slowly, feeling sad. "We're doomed to do this over and over you know."

"We've had this conversation a couple of times." He growled.

She looked at him. He was staring intently out over the dead brown grass. It was autumn already on the High Plane. If he had been in cat form his tail would have been twitching. She put a hand on his arm.

"Sorry. I know we think alike. Most of us on the side do..."

She let her vision widen to include the line of immortals past him. Waiting patiently to run screaming out into the field of battle and inflict pain and damage on one another. Only to do it again and again.

Sometimes she wondered if the humans had it inverted. This was hell, not heaven.

She looked back out to where the generals were riding back to the lines. Heff didn't look happy. She lifted a hand in salute to him and he veered over to cross the lines where they were.

"We go at them in the same old way?" She greeted him.

"I've just spent two hours trying to convince them otherwise. And the last three months..."

She could hear his fatigue and see it in the slump of his shoulders. She patted his leg. The unicorn he was riding reached around to nip at her hair and she swatted him affectionately. Heff managed a little smile.

"As much as this sucks, using the back-up weapon would be worse." She stretched to loosen any kinks, preparing herself for combat. "Maybe our victory up here will satisfy them down there."

Heff nodded. "That's my hope, too. Otherwise..." He looked across at the lines of beings. "This is just stupid."

"We're ready when you are, General, to fight and even die if need be."

He looked sharply down at her, caught by her phrasing.

"That's a mixed blessing." He replied gruffly. She knew he didn't want to do it either, not this battle, but especially not the weapon they now had below. He nodded at Steve, who nodded back. Then he rode off without a backward look, his back straight and unwavering.

Sekhmet sighed. "Let's do this," she muttered to herself. Scooping up her helmet, she slid it on over the cushioning braids she and Steve had done that morning. She stole a look at him. He was always so focused before a battle, but this morning they had been able to forget it all in her tent, shut away from this reality.

She squared her shoulders and stepped into the chariot, nodding curtly at her driver and stringing her bow. She had adopted the Hyksos style of war more millennia ago than she cared to recall. This was something that fit her like a well-worn boot. The dual natured goddess shed the last remnant of the gentle Hathor and became fully the embodiment of wrath and vengeance.

She drew her short sword and held it high. The sun glinted off hers and hundreds of other blades that would ride or run at her side.

"Aduro!" she bellowed. This had all started with Hephaestus, after all. With his imprisonment of his mother until she agreed to free him. And he had showed them all a way to live, not just to rule with iron power. All up and down the line, her cry was echoed. Truly, they were about to burn...

The chariot rocketed forward, Sekhmet moving easily with the motion, completely in balance. She sheathed the sword and nocked her first arrow, waiting...

The lines drew near one another, screaming in so many languages that none could be heard. She was far ahead of her own lines. She lined the arrow up with an immortal she recognized and let fly. She could hear the hiss of the arrow for a second, and then a moment later, Mars' scream as it took his eye out.

"That's for my children, you cretin!" she screamed, and then she was past and shooting for all she was worth.

30

QUANTUM TRAVEL

*L*inn found feeding to hungry goblins to be very satisfying. They were no messier about eating than the kittens, at least. When lunch had been consumed, Daffyd told her they were almost finished preparing the weapon.

"Go ahead and break camp, Linn." He gripped her shoulder as she still sat on the ground. "We just need to install the warhead. With the solid-state fuel, there wasn't a lot of deterioration. And you can help us move it outside, so it will be ready to launch if it's needed."

"What about this fog? Is it going to clear?"

"Not just yet. Should be alarming the personnel at Dillingham, though. There is never fog on the North Shore."

Linn shook her head. She hadn't known that. "Great. Now the humans will be looking into it, which will make the immortals curious."

"Ach, don't worry. They have no idea what Naiads can do. Or the coblyns, for that matter. We came to this plane as servants. They ignore us rogues now." He grinned, displaying sharp little teeth.

"I'll get ready." Linn promised. When they had gone back into the bunker she policed the area, making sure no traces remained of their brief stay. The tent that had been erected outside the shelter was still up, but she let the tent remain for the time. With its shelter she was at least able to pretend to be dry even after the bunker had been resealed.

Blackie, who had been going onto forays into the woods, popped his head into the tent again.

"Hey, there. What have you been up to?"

He opened his mouth, closed it again, and then growled softly, deep in his throat. Alarmed, Linn got up. "What's wrong?"

She followed him into the fog. He led her away from the bunker the coblyns were working in. She had to trot to keep up with him, Lambent slapping against her thigh.

"Wait up!" She called to him. He was almost out of sight. Blackie stopped and looked back at her, his ears flat and tail lashing. She came up to him and placed a hand on his head. "Where are we going?"

He took her wrist gently in his mouth and led her forward. She was immediately aware they were walking up a steep incline. The fog got thicker, if that were possible. Linn drew in her breath. Blackie let go her hand, gave her a searching look, and then started to run. Almost without thought, Linn followed him.

The fog had become almost a tunnel, with tiny flashes of light sparking in her peripheral vision. It was also dark. Blackie could see where he was going, but she couldn't. She unsheathed Lambent and held her up, glowing brightly. She kept running. She didn't dare stop. This had to be the high path the immortals used, and Blackie was generating it.

She'd speculated that the high path was a form of quantum tunneling. That right now, her individual atoms were disassociated and they were running through everything else... Her skin crawled and she suppressed a sob of terror. She didn't have the power to do this. She had to keep up with Blackie.

"Blackie, wait!" She cried out. He slowed and flicked a concerned glance back at her over his shoulder. When had the kitten developed those muscles in his skinny frame? she thought fleetingly. Blackie kept moving. She kept running, Lambent a torch in the dark tunnel. She was acutely aware of the similarity to her dream. But she couldn't stop.

Reality diverged from the dream when she was aware that she was falling. She lost sight of Blackie, but kept Lambent in her hand. She landed and stumbled to her knees and caught herself with her free hand. It was dark here, but the kind of dark that had stars overhead and a moon rising on the horizon.

"Blackie!" She screamed. Holding Lambent over her head she looked for him, feeling a cold wind flick at her face, stinging her cheeks after the humid warmth of Hawaii. She didn't know how far they had traveled.

She couldn't see him in the dark. She stood still, her breath catching in her throat, trying to listen. She could hear the wind hissing through grass... Lowering Lambent, she could see she was standing in a flat, level steppe type of grassland. She looked up at the moon. It wasn't Earth's moon. Rising fast, it was huge and rode low in the sky, lending a pale glow to the land below it. She sheathed Lambent and called Blackie again, softly.

It occurred to her to focus and look for his power. She looked hard... and saw power everywhere. Flickering in patches and flares over the ground in more colors and combinations than she had seen before. Linn gasped and covered her eyes with her hands. She felt dizzy.

She forced herself to look again... Slowly, she looked for the bright blue that was Blackie. The movement caught her eye. There he was, slowly coming toward her. She started toward him, and then tripped over something yielding, landing in a sticky puddle. She looked back and almost screamed.

Flickering a little with muddy red power, there was a body lying there. From the power she knew he had to be an immortal, be he certainly looked dead. One of his arms was missing and there was black blood everywhere. Which is what she'd fallen in. She could smell it now.

Blackie bumped her with his nose and she wrapped her arms around his neck, trying not to cry. "What happened here?" She whispered into his furry ear.

He didn't answer, not that she had expected him to. Instead, he bumped her face with his nose and turned back in the direction he'd come from. She got to her feet and followed him. In the moonlight she could see the sheen on his glossy coat.

She blinked until the power flickers faded from her sight. Now that she knew each of them was a body lying on the plain, she really didn't want to see. She wondered what had happened here. Had this been the battle Grampa Heff was preparing for?

Suddenly she heard a moan and stopped, looking around. She could hear it again... there... where Blackie was. He looked at her with glowing golden eyes and then lowered his head to where someone was lying on the ground. Linn ran forward, dropping to her knees next to the injured immortal.

Blackie was washing his face clean. Linn nudged him aside and looked down into Bes's face. She gasped.

Bess opened his eyes and looked up. "Aduro," he whispered unseeing, then closed his eyes again. Linn started to cry. He was terribly wounded, his gut open to the moonlight. She didn't know what an immortal could take, and his power... she focused. Instead of a flare she could barely stand to look at, he was flickering faintly with white.

Linn held her hands over the worst wound and bit her lips. Blackie lowered his nose to touch her crossed hands. A flare of pink mixed with blue erupted from them and arced into Bes' body. Linn whimpered. Even with Blackie, that had hurt.

Bes opened his eyes again. This time he was focusing. He stared up at them for a minute. Linn realized it was too dark for him to see her face. She slid Lambent out of her sheath and into her lap. The glow reflected off her face and she leaned over him, trying to smile.

"Bes?"

His eyes widened. "What. The. Hell..." He bit out with anger in his tone. Linn flinched from the rage.

"It's me." She told him hesitantly. Blackie licked his cheek, which was uncharacteristically stubbly. "And Blackie."

"How did you two get here?" Bes whispered. "Is that really you?"

Linn could see the pain on his face. She wondered if she could do the power transfer thing again. She wasn't sure what it did, but it seemed to have been helpful.

"Blackie brought me. I think it was the high path. We were just about done with..." She hesitated, not knowing who might still be listening "What we were working on." She finished, feeling lame about that last answer

"You ran the high path." he repeated, looking stunned. He tried to lift a hand. Linn took it in hers. He was cold... she bit her lips in concern.

"Blackie..." She looked at her companion. "Can we do it again?"

"Do what again?" Bes asked. She ignored him for the moment. Blackie moved around to the other side and extended his head over Bes' body. Linn leaned over from the other side. They touched foreheads.

This time the glow of their power lasted a full minute. Twisting strands of blue and pink extended down into Bes and Linn could see his skin move and the wound closing. Then she started to pass out. Throwing herself to the side so she wouldn't fall onto Bes, her world dissolved into gray sparkling nothingness, and then to black.

She woke staring up at the moon, Blackie licking her face. She tried to sit up and fell back, too dizzy to manage. she turned her head and could see that she was inches from Bes. He was looking at her with a funny expression on his face. Still flat on his back, but the pain and tension had eased. She grayed out again. Bes was saying something, but she couldn't make it out.

After a minute... or more, Linn couldn't tell, she started to feel again. She hadn't been completely out that time. It was more like she'd stepped away from her body for a minute. She took a deep breath, feeling her head spinning. She gagged. The smell on the battlefield was bad and getting worse.

"Linn! Linn..." Bes' urgent whisper got through to her. She opened her eyes and saw him trying to sit up.

"No!" She pushed herself up. He slumped back.

"Look..." He tried to point, his hand shaking.

She looked across his body at Blackie, who was standing, his face contorted into a silent snarl, and his back hair standing on end. Linn staggered to her feet, Lambent in hand. Advancing toward them were three beings, black power boiling off them like a fog.

She faced them, Lambent in hand, feeling a snarl on her face as well. As they came closer, she could see they walked on all fours, with a curious, limping gait. They stopped as they saw her, whining a little like dogs. One of them lifted his heavy head and sniffed the air.

He laughed, a long, high pitched chattering howl that set Linn's teeth on edge.

"How... Delicious." He said in that high voice. "Look, my dears, a halfling and a kitten stand to protect our greatest enemy."

All three of the hyenas started to laugh as they walked toward Linn and Blackie. Bes was still helpless on the ground. Linn cried out in fear. The miasma that surrounded them stank like long-dead flesh.

"Stop!" she screamed at them. "Go away from here!"

They stopped and whined, slinking low to the ground. "Hehe...the child wants us to be gone." one said.

"Wants us to let her be..." Another hissed.

"But we are so hungry..." the leader whimpered. "We want their juicy flesh."

"Come closer and I'll kill you." Linn stated grimly, her jaw set.

"Oh, oooh..." Moaned one, sinking to the ground and covering his face with his paws. Then he looked up, laughing. Linn could see the flash of his teeth in his open jaws.

"We are already dead..." He choked out. Next to her, Blackie snarled a warning. The other two were trying to flank them.

"Zombie hyenas. What next?" Linn muttered. "At least I can hurt you." she lunged, slashing with Lambent like she was swinging an axe. The glowing sword bit into the back of the leader's neck with a meaty thunk. He screamed a howl, hurling himself backward.

Linn, who had twisted the sword out as she struck, rocked back on the balls or her feet, seeing the other lunge at her, but Blackie leapt and bit deep in his throat, rolling him across the bloody plain. She let them go and pivoted toward the third hyena. He was slinking toward her. She shrieked and ran at him, swinging Lambent high over her head and then down at his skull. He tried to roll out of the way, and she slashed his throat open and one of his forelegs off entirely.

His high scream was almost human, and then he turned tail and ran across the plain. Linn didn't chase him, spinning instead to see the hyena Blackie had bitten break free and run away, too. The leader was nowhere in sight. Linn held Lambent high, flaring bright with power, and walked around Bes' prone body, making sure they were really gone. The sword, covered in blood and bone bits, crackled and hissed.

Satisfied, she knelt and wiped the blade as clean as she could with a tuft of dry grass. She didn't want that nasty stuff on her sword. Breathing deeply and trying to let the rage that had been coursing through her flow out again, she went to Bes.

Bending over him, she touched his forehead. His eyes were closed again. They fluttered open at her touch. He was warmer. She pulled her trembling hand back.

He gave her a little smile. "You are magnificent."

Linn raised an eyebrow. "You're delusional."

He chuffed out a breath that might have been a laugh. "They won't come back. Much easier prey than us out there tonight."

Linn felt her shoulders relax. She had been so tensed it hurt. "All right."

She pulled off her jacket, shivering a little in the wind. She hadn't brought her pack. She made a mental not to never leave it again. Twice, now, she had been caught without it. Spreading the thin windbreaker over Bes' torso, she patted her pockets.

Back in Hawaii... however far away that was, now... she'd put a mylar wrap in her cargo pocket, in case it got cold enough that night to need it against the damp conditions. She'd been hypothermic once and that was enough. She stretched it out, now, knowing the thin layer of plastic would help keep him from losing anymore body heat, at least.

She tucked it around him, ignoring his murmured protestations. Blackie reappeared and stretched out next to Bes, his tongue lolling out. She nodded at him.

"You ok?" she asked.

He nodded back, then put his big head on Bes' shoulder. Linn realized that he was as long as the short man, stretched out like this. She stood up and looked around again. The moon was high overhead now, thin clouds racing across the surface. She could see dark shapes huddled on the ground here and there.

There was no sign of the hyenas. She refocused, drawing upon her Sight. She sucked in a quick breath. Off to one side, far enough away she couldn't make out details, there was a flare of golden power. She drew Lambent again and stood over Bes, remembering not to lock her knees.

"What is it?" he asked.

"I don't know. Just... a lot of power."

Now there was another flare, near where the first one had been, but this one was a pale blue. Linn swore, tensing. Bes, below her, chuckled hoarsely.

"Better not let anyone else hear you say things like that."

She glanced down at him, seeing the smile on his face. "Glad you're feeling better. At least down there validates your low sense of humor."

He tried to suppress the laughter this time, as it obviously hurt. She was pleased that he was laughing, though, and back closer to normal.

The flares happened again, closer. Linn could see people walking, now, and... she squinted. A horse-drawn wagon?

"Bes?" she asked quietly, not looking at him. She didn't dare look away from the approaching group.

"Yes, Linn?" He had an odd note to his voice.

"Who is the enemy here, and how do I tell?"

"Ah..." he sighed. "There is a question I could spend years on."

"A quick answer would be good." She shot back drily.

"Try shouting 'Aduro' when they draw near." He sounded better, she noted absently. Whatever she and Blackie had done, it must have worked. Blackie...

Linn looked down. Blackie was asleep, his paws twitching in a dream. Fat lot of help he was. "Blackie!" she hissed urgently at him. He sat up, yawning. His ears twitched toward the approaching group of people. They stopped, and there was another flare of golden power.

Blackie jumped to his feet and took off.

"Dammit, Cat!" Linn shouted hoarsely after him. She looked back down at Bes, torn. Did she leave him, who still couldn't move, or go after the idiot kitten?

She stayed where she was. The group bunched up when Blackie bounded into them, and then started to move toward her, fast. In the moonlight she still couldn't make out details. There were, she thought, six of them coming toward her. The rest were staying with the wagon, which had stopped.

She had been holding Lambent loosely at her side, and now she swung her up, power flaring off the tip as she did so. Bracing herself over Bes, she screamed defiantly.

"Aduro!"

Bes shouted weakly beneath her. Linn bared her teeth and prepared to die. She had no illusions about her chances against immortals. They had started to run, now, and suddenly they shouted back to her.

"Aduro! Aduro!"

The power flared from all of them... Red, green, gold, blue, iridescent, and the pure yellow that was Sekhmet. Sobbing, Linn dropped Lambent and ran to meet them. She cried out as she recognized the golden woman.

"Mama! Mama..." She fell into Theta's arms. Sobbing wildly, she couldn't have stopped crying if she had wanted to. Burying her face in her mother's embrace, Linn clung to her for a second.

Her face wet with tears, she looked up at her mother. "Bes... Bes is hurt."

Her mother was crying too, Linn realized. She just nodded and let Linn go, hurrying toward Bes. Grandfather caught hold of her now, kissing her forehead.

"How the hell did you get here?!" He demanded, squeezing her.

Linn gurgled a little laugh. "Bes asked me that, too. Blackie brought me."

Sekhmet squeezed her shoulder. "You looked ready for trouble there. Anything we should know?"

Linn shook her head, suddenly very tired. "There were zombie hyenas. I think they are gone, now."

Quetzalcoatl kissed her cheek tenderly and she felt a jump of power from him. "Brave little girl." Was all he said.

Coyote strolled up to her. He hugged her and led her to meet the member of the party she hadn't met. The blue lady was a tall, dark-haired woman with a prominent nose and a broad smile.

"I am Panacea." She held out her hands and Linn took them, feeling warm, soft skin.

"The Greek goddess of healing." Linn said softly, wondering why she was with Grandpa Heff, she was an old one, and shouldn't be on his side.

Panacea nodded. "After battles, I roam the field helping the fallen ones recover."

"Bes is hurt." Linn told her, looking over to where her mother was kneeling at Bes' side. She walked over and knelt on the other side of him. They had stopped talking when she came near. "What?" She asked.

"Bes was just telling me how you and Blackie were trying to heal him." her mother had a little quiver in her voice.

Linn looked at her numbly. "Did I do it wrong? She asked, suddenly alarmed.

"No, no..." Theta bit her lip. Linn recognized that. She did it herself when worried.

"What is wrong?" her voice squeaked a little.

"Hey, there." Bes spoke, lifting a hand to her. She took it automatically, squeezing it a little. He did it to calm her, and it worked.

"It's just that it was very dangerous for you to do." her mother told her. "Healing is a huge power drain. I'm tapping into all the power I've drained from volcanoes over the course of months, Panacea has been charging herself for years..."

"Oh." Linn looked down at Bes. He had that look on his face again. "I didn't think about it, Mom. I just..." She fluttered her hands, trying to put into words the way she'd felt when she looked down and saw him lying there broken and split open.

Bes grunted and tried to push himself up. Both Linn and Theta grabbed him by the shoulders. Theta looked at Linn. "Do. Not. Try. To. Help." She snapped. Then she flared.

Linn felt like she was wrapped in golden flames. Warmth slid through her skin, into her bones. She looked into Bes' face, seeing his eyes closed and a tear sliding down his cheek. The world slowed to a crawl and the expression on his face was of agony and joy all at once. The flames snapped out and he sat up, wrapping his arms around her.

Linn was crying again, into Bes' solid shoulder. She was sitting awry on the cold, hard ground, her arms wrapped around him. He was petting her hair. "Shhh. shhh... let it out now."

She hiccupped and he chuckled. "Can we get up now?" He asked with a mixture of laughter and tenderness in his voice.

She scrambled to her feet, sniffing and looking for her handkerchief. That, at least, she hadn't left behind. Her grandfather, smiling, extended a hand to Bes. They clasped forearms and the burly smith pulled the shorter immortal to his feet. Bes stretched and groaned.

"Thank you, Theta." He hugged her briefly.

Coyote handed Lambent to Linn. She smiled at him. Her face felt stiff with fatigue and tears dried onto it. She was covered in blood and mud from the run throughout the field and her fight. But everything was all right. Blackie bumped her hand with his head. She cupped his furry skull in her fingers.

"Can we go home now?" She asked softly.

"Yes, you can. Which home to you want to go to?" her mother asked her very gently.

31

HOMEWARD BOUND

*L*inn blinked at her mother. She realized this was a choice... the apartment in Seattle, or the Sanctuary. Suddenly she knew that if she chose the apartment, she wouldn't remember all this. She could go back to the shallow girl she had been on the plane that summer, just killing time waiting for life to go back to normal. None of this would seem real, just a bad dream she'd awakened from.

Linn drew a deep breath and squared her shoulders. There was something she still needed to do before she could be safely at home, wherever that was. "I left the coblyns at the bunker in Hawaii. I need to get back there and help them get home."

Theta blinked at her, then slowly smiled. She looked at Heff without speaking. He grinned broadly. Then he looked at Bes.

"Feel up to taking her?"

"Not baby-sitting this time." The Egyptian growled.

"No, not anymore." Heff agreed with a chuckle.

Bes looked at Linn, his eyes clear and dark. No power shone there to conceal his soul. "Want me to come along?" He asked her.

"Of course." she replied. "I have no idea how to get back there."

He laughed, that full belly laugh she hadn't heard in too long.

"Right then. Ready?"

"Just a minute." She told him tranquilly. Then she hugged everyone, ending with her mother.

"Will you come to Sanctuary? Bring Grampa?" she whispered.

"Of course." Her mother whispered back in her ear. "Couldn't keep me away, love."

Linn sniffed and stepped away. "Ok, now I'm ready." She told her companions

Bes took her hand and Blackie flanked her. They started to run and the moonlit land tunneled out and away. They were back on the high path. Bes didn't move as fast as Blackie had done, before. Linn thought Blackie must have known Bes was in trouble, before. Maybe he'd been coming here every time he disappeared into the fog.

They landed much more smoothly, as Bes had talked her through how to do it as they jogged along on the tunnel. She'd told him where they were going, and he told her how to land with bended knees for more bounce.

The fog was still laying over the landscape like a wet blanket. Linn sucked in a lungful of warm, wet air, catching the exotic scents and sea air. She pulled her compass out and consulted it, looking at the ground. She figured if she found the cattle path, she could get back to camp.

Bes swept her a little bow. "Lead on!"

She nodded wanly. All the activity was catching up with her. She really wanted a nap and food, not necessarily in that order. By the time she got them into camp she was shaking a little.

Bes sat her down and put her jacket over her. It seemed odd to Linn that nothing had changed here since she left. Her pack was all put together and leaning against the pole of the lean-to. The little green fire was still flickering merrily. She held her hands out to it, and then snatched them back, not wanting Bes to see how they were trembling.

He pulled open the small pouch on her backpack and handed her a protein bar and then the spout of her camelbak. "Eat and drink. You put a lot of yourself into me..." his eyes softened. "Using that much power means you need to refuel. This will help."

Linn just nodded, too tired to speak. She chewed slowly. It tasted delicious, which probably meant she was pretty bad off. Normally the protein bars were disgusting. He stood up.

"I'm going to go check in with the coblyns. I will be right back, Ok?"

"I'll be here." Which was true, Linn reflected, because she didn't have the energy to go with him. Once they had gotten safely back to Earth, it was like someone had opened a tap and emptied her out. She took another bite.

She was half asleep when he came back. She was aware that he was there, but too tired to speak to him. He talked to her anyway.

"They are almost done. It's ready to launch when Heff sends word. Daffyd wants me to take you straight back to the Sanctuary."

"How...?" she managed.

"Since we don't know when launch will be, and maybe we'll never need it at all, they need a stronger look-don't-see spell. I'm going to send Coyote to them. He can set concealment and get them home."

Linn closed her eyes. She didn't want to go anywhere; she was too tired to move. Bes shook her shoulder. "Come on, Linn. Let's go home."

"There's an offer I can't refuse..." She muttered. She still didn't move.

Bes scooped her up. Linn squeaked. "You can't carry me!"

"I can and you aren't moving..." He started to walk, and she knew without opening her eyes they were back on the high path. She relaxed and let herself drift into sleep. She felt safe again.

Linn woke up in her own bed at the Sanctuary. She rubbed her eyes and sat up. She had been undressed and was in a baggy tee and her underwear. She had not been cleaned up, though. She looked at her hands and could see traces of the blood from the battlefield.

"Ugh." She rolled out of bed and staggered into the bathroom. She felt like she had been hit with a stick. Several times, by someone who meant it. She stood for a long time under the hot water, washing twice to get off the mud and blood, and that helped. Clean fresh clothes helped too. Linn decided that food would make everything better.

The common room was busy. She wasn't sure what time it was... she'd taken off her watch in disgust and left it in the bathroom until she could stand to clean the yuck off it.

Stopping in the doorway, Linn sniffed. It smelled like lunch.

She cleared her throat. "Dierdre?" she asked the empty air, feeling awkward. She wondered if that would ever feel normal.

The little Coblyn appeared at her elbow. Linn jumped. "Good grief! How did you do that?"

Dierdre chuckled at Linn's reaction. "I was right here, don't worry. We can't teleport."

"Oh, that's good to hear. I was wondering..." Linn stopped and felt awkward. "How long was I asleep?"

"Bes brought you in in last night. It's a little later than noon, now... Hungry?"

Linn nodded. "Very. Thank you."

Gareth, tail high, romped up to her. Linn bent down and hugged him. Like his brother, he was too big to pick up. Blackie had grown bigger than the grey tabby, though. It felt weird to be here, now. She kept thinking about the battlefield and trying to reconcile the cold, dead place with this warm, happy room. Deirdre touched her elbow.

"You ok?" There was concern in her big, dark green eyes.

"Not... really." Linn admitted.

"Food first, and then let's talk, ok?" Deirdre took her hand and towed the larger girl toward a table.

"All right."

Linn let Deirdre pick out the food, she really didn't care what it was. When she was eating, she stopped long enough to ask if Bes and Blackie were at the Sanctuary.

"Blackie hasn't come back yet. Bes is in the Library."

Linn thought about that while she finished. Blackie must have stayed with the coblyns, she didn't remember him when they came back to the Sanctuary. He would be all right with them, Daffyd would take care of him. Bes... she wanted to talk to Bes.

Deirdre came around and hugged her. Linn, surprised, wrapped her arms around the tiny Coblyn. She smelled spicy and her hair was soft.

"Go on. I'll take your plate up, and tonight your grandparents and mother will be back."

"Great." Linn sat up. "Is Hypatia in her office?"

Deirdre rolled her eyes, making Linn smile. "Always. Want to take her lunch to her?"

"Sure." The familiar chore would be good, she thought.

Linn carried a plate down the tunnel hall to Hypatia's office. Had it really only been three days ago she was sitting in this office trying to figure out how to make the Nikes work for the EMP warhead?

She knocked on the door.

"Enter." That papery voice hadn't changed at all. Even if Linn felt very different inside, the outside was the same.

Hypatia didn't look up from the book she held as Linn placed the plate by her elbow. "Thank you, dear." She murmured.

Linn smiled and went back out of the office. She'd talk to Hypatia later, when she had her attention. The gray tunnel reminded her of the high path. She wondered if the coblyns had done that on purpose. She pushed open one half of the double door into the library.

Standing on the threshold she inhaled the unique scent of old books and other things she couldn't identify. Hypatia had told her the faint spiciness was myrrh. All Linn knew was that the first time she had come in here she'd felt at home. She made her way to the center of the library.

Bes was sitting on the semi-circular couch with a paperback in his hand. He looked up at her approach. "Here you are... How are you feeling?"

"Better." Linn sat down next to him. "I feel weird."

He put the book down. "Understandable. You saw a lot. Did a lot. Most of it outside the realm of what you considered reality not too long ago."

"Yeah." She curled up, kicking her sandals off so her feet could be on the leather, and hugged her knees. "I mean, I like being here. I'm ok with what you are, and Mom, and my grandparents."

"Of course. Your family loves you, and it's getting bigger all the time."

Linn thought of Dierdre's hug. "It is." She felt herself smile even though she didn't really feel like it.

"Life is good." Bes went on. "You know I've seen it all. The bad parts, the happy moments."

She nodded. The white fire was back in his eyes. He predated the human race, she knew that, she just forgot it from time to time.

"You look younger." She blurted. Then she blushed at what she'd just said. But it was true. The old man who'd showed up at Grampa Heff's farm was now maybe middle-aged.

Bes threw his head back and roared with laughter.

"I can look whatever age I want to." He managed after a moment. "You told me once before it was silly for me to pretend to be old."

"Yeah... I'd forgotten, actually." Linn admitted.

"Want me to change back?"

"No..." She looked at him. Dark hair looked better on him than the salt and pepper.

"So, tomorrow everyone comes back here." He commented, picking his book up. The same author as the dragon book he'd been reading before, she noted.

"Yeah... What about the missile?"

"That's Heff's back up plan if they should come for us here. We don't think so, usually the battle soothes their blood lust, but they have been acting out of character in places. Like the attack on the children."

Linn shivered, suddenly picturing the little ones lying limp and scattered lit the bodies on the battlefield. "I couldn't bear it if something happened to them."

"Nothing will happen to them." He assured her.

"Something happened to you..." She bit her lip.

"I'm an immortal."

"Bad things happen to immortals too. The twins taught me that." The thought of the children and their mother trapped into a living hell bothered her. She'd asked again and again if there was anything that could be done. Pele and Hypatia had both told her there was nothing...

She shivered again. "This weapon could easily hurt my family, not just my enemies." She said slowly.

Bes reached over and put his fingertip on her nose. "I think..." he started.

"What?" Linn wriggled her nose. His fingertip was callused, but not too rough.

"You should go let the Naiads teach you how to surf."

"I don't feel like it." She protested; her mind still caught on the impact of what she had done with helping create the EMP.

"Ah!" He raised the finger to stop her. "Go on, have fun, wear yourself out. It will help. And then we can talk later, or you can talk to your mother when she gets here."

Linn sighed. "Ok. I'll do it."

He picked his book up again. "Such a hardship," he murmured into it with a grin.

Linn stuck her tongue out at him and went back to her room for her suit.

She was lying on a surfboard, letting the sun soak into her skin when he mother called her name. She had been up on it several times, and fallen, and tried again... Surfing wasn't as easy as it looked, but it had been fun and she had forgotten to think for a while.

"Mom!" Linn waved, and started to paddle toward shore. Her mother dropped her wrap-around and waded out into the water. Linn met her when she was waist deep and straddled the board, hugging Theta.

"I have missed you so much." Theta told her.

"Me too." Linn sighed. "Mom?"

"Yeah, honey?" Theta smiled at her, brilliant in the sunshine.

"Can we stay here?"

"Well, I think our toes would get all pruny after a while. And I'm hungry, I was hoping you'd join me for dinner."

"Mom! That's not what I meant!" Linn laughed. This felt so good, her mom here, her family all in one place for the first time.

"I don't see why we couldn't live here as well as in Seattle." Theta's eyes sparkled.

"Oh, yay!" Linn threw her arms back around her mother, squeezing hard.

"I love you too, punkin." Her mother bent her head over her and kissed her on the forehead, then let go.

Theta dove into the waves. Linn slipped off the board and swam with her for a while. The naiads splashed in the waves and Linn realized when they were wading out that she hadn't thought about the battlefield all afternoon.

Pele was waiting on the sand for them, holding towels. She hugged them both at once, heedless of the water. "I am so happy to have both my girls here at once." She crowed. Linn guessed that she knew, but blurted it out anyway.

"Mom says we can live in Hawaii!" Linn bounced a little.

Pele laughed. "Oh, that makes me so happy! Theta..." She hugged her daughter again. "Will you stay here, in the Sanctuary?"

"For now, at least, mother."

"Where is Grampa?" Linn asked. Pele pointed up at the terrace. Linn saw him standing there, dressed in an eye-bleeding Hawaiian shirt and baggy shorts. She waved and started to run to him.

He met her on the path, hugging and holding her fiercely. "Linnaea. I'm so sorry... I wanted to keep you safe and..." he trailed off.

"Grampa... this isn't bad. I'm ok... almost everyone is ok. The children are safe. Mom says we can live here. Will you stay here?" She blurted everything that was on her mind out all at once.

He grinned. "Well, Bes tells me my cabin is toothpicks. I guess I don't have anywhere else for a while."

Linn whooped and tore down the path back to Pele and Theta.

"Mom! Mom! Guess what!" She felt like she had wings as she ran to tell them that the family was whole again.

Heff stared after her. He wished it would be so easy to feel happy for him. There were too many threats still looming, though. And the curious power of Coyote's monster, the great Dragon who was dead and yet spoke, tickled at the back of his brain. An umber cloud seemed to pass in front of his eyes.

"Home... I desssire... Home." The echo of power in the Dragon's sibilant voice.

Heff whispered it aloud, knowing that he was privileged to be in a state the monster desired. "I'm home."

He headed down the path to the beach, wanting nothing more than to hold his family all in his arms at once. Tomorrow or the next day he'd worry.

ABOUT THE AUTHOR

Cedar Sanderson was born a military brat and spent her childhood moving to new duty stations. Her formative years after her father left the Air Force were spent being home-schooled on the Alaskan frontier. She is a scientist, while running a household, an art and design business, and writing multiple novels on the side with occasional forays into coloring books and children's stories. She has written more short stories than she can keep track of, and the recent publication of *The Case of the Perambulating Hatrack* makes her tenth novel in print. She also has a blog with over a decade of essays, recipes, and artwork for you to explore should you so desire at www.cedarwrites.com. In any case, writing seems to be a compulsion for her; she's not planning to give up any time soon.

ALSO BY CEDAR SANDERSON

God's Wolfling

Crow Moon

Tanager's Fledglings

www.ingramcontent.com/pod-product-compliance
Lightning Source LLC
Chambersburg PA
CBHW070749180626
46818CB00007B/3042